'You're not the only one who can read people, you know.'

'You can read me?' Chase leaned forward, his eyes glinting in the candlelight.

She saw the golden-brown stubble on his jaw, could almost feel its sandpaper roughness under her fingers. She breathed in the scent of him: part musk, part sun, pure male.

'What am I thinking now?' he asked—a steely, softly worded challenge.

Millie didn't dare answer.

She knew what *she* was thinking. She was thinking about taking that hard jaw between her hands and angling her lips over his. His lips would be soft but firm, commanding and drawing deep from her. And she would give—she would surrender that long-held part of herself in just one kiss. She knew it—felt it bone-deep. Soul-deep. Which was ridiculous, because she barely knew this man. Yet in the space of an hour or two he'd drawn more from her than anyone had since her husband's death, or even before. He'd seen more, glimpsed her sadness and subterfuge as no one else could or had. No one had seen through her smoke and mirrors. No one but Chase.

And he was a *stranger*.

A stranger who could kiss her quite senseless.

Kate Hewitt discovered her first Mills & Boon®
romance on a trip to England when she was thirteen,
and she's continued to read them ever since. She wrote
her first story at the age of five, simply because her
older brother had written one and she thought she
could do it too. That story was one sentence long—
fortunately they've become a bit more detailed as she's
grown older. She has written plays, short stories and
magazine serials for many years, but writing romance
remains her first love. Besides writing, she enjoys
reading, travelling and learning to knit.

After marrying the man of her dreams—her older
brother's childhood friend—she lived in England for
six years, and now resides in Connecticut with her
husband, her three young children, and the possibility
of one day getting a dog.

Kate loves to hear from readers—you can contact her
through her website: www.kate-hewitt.com

Recent titles by the same author:

THE HUSBAND SHE NEVER KNEW
THE DARKEST OF SECRETS
KHOLODOV'S LAST MISTRESS
MR AND MISCHIEF *(The Powerful and the Pure)*

BENEATH THE
VEIL OF PARADISE

BY
KATE HEWITT

First published in Great Britain 2012
by Mills & Boon, an imprint of Harlequin (UK) Limited.
Harlequin (UK) Limited, Eton House, 18-24 Paradise Road,
Richmond, Surrey TW9 1SR

© Kate Hewitt 2012

ISBN: 978 0 263 22824 3

Harlequin (UK) policy is to use papers that are natural, renewable
and recyclable products and made from wood grown in sustainable
forests. The logging and manufacturing process conform to the
legal environmental regulations of the country of origin.

Printed and bound in Great Britain
by CPI Antony Rowe, Chippenham, Wiltshire

BENEATH THE
VEIL OF PARADISE

CHAPTER ONE

WAS she ever going to start painting?

The woman had been sitting and staring at the blank canvas for the better part of an hour. Chase Bryant had been watching her, nursing his drink at the ocean-side bar and wondering if she'd ever actually put brush to paper, or canvas, as the case might be.

She didn't.

She was fussy; he could see that straight off. She was in a luxury resort on a remote island in the Caribbean, and her tan capris had knife-edge pleats. Her pale-blue polo shirt looked like she'd ironed it an hour ago. He wondered what she did to relax. If she relaxed. Considering her attitude in their current location, he doubted it.

Still, there was something intriguing about the determined if rather stiff set of her shoulders, the compressed line of her mouth. She wasn't particularly pretty—well, not his kind of pretty anyway, which he fully admitted was lush, curvy blondes. This woman was tall, just a few inches under his own six feet, and angular. He could see the jut of her collarbone, the sharp points of her elbows. She had a narrow face, a forbidding expression, and even her hairstyle was severe, a blunt bob of near black that looked like she trimmed it with nail scissors every week. Its razor-straight edge swung by the strong line of her jaw as she moved.

He'd been watching her since she arrived, her canvas and paints under one arm. She'd set her stuff up on the beach a little way off from the bar, close enough so he could watch her while he sipped his sparkling water. No beers for him on this trip, unfortunately.

She'd been very meticulous about it all, arranging the collapsible easel, the box of paints, the little three-legged stool. Moving everything around until it was all just so, and she was on a beach. In the Caribbean. She looked like she was about to teach an evening art class for over-sixties.

Still he waited. He wondered if she was any good. She had a gorgeous view to paint—the aquamarine sea, a stretch of spun-sugar sand. There weren't even many people to block the view; the resort wasn't just luxurious, it was elite and discreet. He should know. His family owned it. And right now he needed discreet.

She finished arranging everything and sat on the stool, staring out to the sea, her posture perfect, back ramrod-straight. For half an hour. It would have been boring except that he could see her face, and how emotions flickered across it like shadows on water. He couldn't exactly decipher what the emotions were, but she clearly wasn't thinking happy thoughts.

The sun had begun its languorous descent towards the sea, and he decided she must be waiting for the sunset. They were spectacular here; he'd seen three of them already. He liked watching the sun set, felt there was something poetic and apt about all that intense beauty over in an instant. He watched now as the sun slipped lower, its long rays causing the placid surface of the sea to shimmer with a thousand lights, the sky ablaze with myriad streaks of colour, everything from magenta to turquoise to gold.

And still she just sat there.

For the first time Chase felt an actual flicker of annoyance. She'd dragged everything out here; obviously she'd intended to paint something. So why wasn't she doing it? Was she afraid? More likely a perfectionist. And, damn it, he knew now that life was too short to wait for the perfect moment, or even an OK moment. Sometimes you just had to wade into the mire and do it. Live while you could.

Pushing away his drink, he rose from his stool and headed over to Miss Fussy.

Millie did not enjoy feeling like a fool. And it felt foolish and, worse, pathetic, sitting here on a gorgeous beach staring at a blank canvas when she'd obviously come to paint.

She just didn't want to any more.

It had been a stupid idea anyway, the kind of thing you read about in self-help books or women's magazines. She'd read one on the plane to St Julian's, something about being kind to yourself. Whatever. The article had described how a woman had taken up gardening after her divorce and had ended up starting her own landscaping business. Lived her dream after years of marital unhappiness. Inspirational. Impossible. Millie turned away from the canvas.

And found herself staring straight at a man's muscled six-pack abs. She looked up and saw a dark-haired Adonis smiling down at her.

'I've heard about watching paint dry, but this is ridiculous.'

Perfect, a smart ass. Millie rose from her stool so she was nearly eye-level. 'As you can see, there's no paint.'

'What are you waiting for?'

'Inspiration,' she answered and gave him a pointed look. 'I'm not finding any here.'

If she'd been trying to offend or at least annoy him, she'd failed. He just laughed, slow and easy, and gave her a thorough once-over with his dark bedroom eyes.

Millie stood taut and still, starting to get angry. She hated guys like this one: gorgeous, flirtatious, and utterly arrogant. Three strikes against him, as far as she was concerned.

His gaze finally travelled up to her face, and she was surprised and discomfited to see a flicker of what almost looked like sympathy there. 'So really,' he asked, dropping the flirt, 'why haven't you painted anything?'

'It's none of your business.'

'Obviously. But I'm curious. I've been watching you from the bar for nearly an hour. You spent a long time on the set-up, but you've been staring into space for thirty minutes.'

'What are you, some kind of stalker?'

'Nope. Just bored out of my mind.'

She stared at him; tried to figure him out. She'd taken him for a cheap charmer but there was something strangely sincere about the way he spoke. Like he really was curious. And really bored.

Something in the way he waited with those dark eyes and that little half-smile made her answer reluctantly, 'I just couldn't do it.'

'It's been a while?'

'Something like that.' She reached over and started to pack up the paints. No point pretending anything was going to happen today. Or any day. Her painting days were long gone.

He picked up her easel and collapsed it in one neat movement before handing it back. 'May I buy you a drink?'

She liked the 'may', but she still shook her head. 'No thanks.' She hadn't had a drink alone with a man in two years. Hadn't done anything in two years but breathe and work and try to survive. This guy wasn't about to make her change her ways.

'You sure?'

She turned to him and folded her arms as she surveyed

him. He really was annoyingly attractive: warm brown eyes, short dark hair, a chiseled jaw and those nice abs. His board shorts rode low on his hips, and his legs were long and powerful. 'Why,' she asked, 'are you even asking? I'd bet a hundred bucks I'm not your usual type.' Just like he wasn't hers.

'Typecast me already?'

'Easily.'

His mouth quirked slightly. 'Well, you're right, you're not my usual type. Way too tall and, you know—' he gestured around her face, making Millie stiffen '—severe. What's with the hair?'

'The hair?' Instinctively and shamefully she reached up to touch her bobbed hair. 'What about it?'

'It's scary. Like, Morticia Addams scary.'

'Morticia *Addams*? Of the Addams Family? She had long hair.' She could not believe they were discussing her hair, and in relation to a television show.

'Did she? Well, maybe I'm thinking of someone else. Somebody with hair like yours. Really sharp-cut.' He made a chopping motion along his own jaw.

'You're being ridiculous. And offensive.' Yet strangely she found herself smiling. She liked his honesty.

He raised his eyebrows. 'So, dinner?'

'I thought it was a drink.'

'Based on the fact that you're still talking to me, I upped the ante.'

She laughed, reluctant, rusty, yet still a laugh. This annoying, arrogant, attractive man amused her somehow. When was the last time she'd actually laughed, had felt like laughing? And she was on holiday—admittedly enforced, but she had a whole week to kill. Seven days was looking like a long time from here. Why not amuse herself? Why not prove she really was moving on, just like her boss Jack had urged her to do? She gave a little decisive nod. 'OK, to the drink only.'

'Are you *haggling*?'

Interest flared; deals she could do. 'What's your counter offer?'

He cocked his head, his gaze sweeping slowly over her once more. And she reacted to that gaze, a painful mix of attraction and alarm. Dread and desire. Hot and cold. A welter of emotions that penetrated her numbness, made her *feel*.

'Drink, dinner, and a walk on the beach.'

Awareness pulsed with an electric jolt low in her belly. 'You were supposed to offer something less, not more.'

His slow, wicked smile curled her toes—and other parts of her person, parts that hadn't curled in a long time. 'I know.'

She hesitated. She should back off, tell him to forget it, yet somehow now that felt like failure. She could handle him. She needed to be able to handle him.

'Fine.' She was agreeing because it was a challenge, not because she wanted to. She liked to set herself little challenges, tests of emotional and physical endurance: *I can jog three miles in eighteen-and-a-half minutes and not even be out of breath. I can look at this photo album for half an hour and not cry.*

Smiling, he reached for the canvas she clutched to her chest. 'Let me carry that for you.'

'Chivalrous of you, but there's no need.' She strode over to the rubbish bin on the edge of the beach and tossed the canvas straight in. The paints, easel and stool followed.

She didn't look at him as she did it, but she felt herself flush. She was just being practical, but she could see how it might seem kind of…severe.

'You are one scary lady.'

She glanced at him, eyebrows raised, everything prickling. 'Are you still talking about my hair?'

'The whole package. But don't worry, I like it.' He grinned and she glared.

'I wasn't worried.'

'The thing I like about you,' he said as he strolled towards the bar, 'is you're so easy to rile.'

Millie had no answer to that one. She *was* acting touchy, but she felt touchy. She didn't do beaches, or bars, or dates. She didn't relax. For the last two years she had done nothing but work, and sunbathing on the beach with a paperback and MP3 player was akin to having her fingernails pulled out one by one. At least that wouldn't take a whole week.

The man—she realised she didn't even know his name—had led her through the beach-side bar to an artful arrangement of tables right on the sand. Each one was shaded by its own umbrella, with comfortable, cushioned chairs and a perfect view of the sea.

The waiter snapped right to attention, so Millie guessed the man was known around here. Probably a big spender. Trust-fund baby or bond trader? Did it matter?

'What's your name?' she asked as she sat across from him. He was gazing out at the sea with a strangely focused look. The orange streaks were like vivid ribbons across the sky. He snapped his attention back to her.

'Chase.'

'Chase.' She gave a short laugh. 'Sounds appropriate.'

'Actually, I don't generally do much chasing.' He gave her a slow, oh-so-sexy smile that had annoyance flaring through her even as her toes—and other parts—curled again.

'Charming, Chase. Do you practise that in the mirror?'

'Practise what?'

'Your smile.'

He laughed and leaned back in his chair. 'Nope, never. But it must be a pretty nice smile, if you think I practise.' He eyed her consideringly. 'Although, the more likely possibility is that you just think you I'm an arrogant ass who's far too full of himself.'

Now she laughed in surprise. She hadn't expected him to be so honest. 'And I could probably tell you what you think of me.'

He arched one eyebrow. 'And that is?'

'Uptight, prissy know-it-all who doesn't know how to have a good time.' As soon as she said the words, she regretted them. This wasn't a conversation she wanted to have.

'Actually, I don't think that.' He remained relaxed, but his gaze swept over her searchingly, making Millie feel weirdly revealed. 'Admittedly, on the surface, yes, I see it. Totally, to a tee. But underneath…' She rolled her eyes, waiting for the come-on. Everything was a chat-up line to a guy like this. 'You seem sad.'

She tensed mid-eye-roll, her gaze arrowing on him. A little smile played around his mouth, drawing attention to those full, sculpted lips. Lips that were lush enough to belong to a woman, yet still seemed intensely masculine. And it was those lips that had so softly issued that scathing indictment.

You seem sad.

'I don't know what you're talking about.' As far as comebacks went, it sucked. And her voice sounded horribly brittle. But Millie didn't have anything better. Averting her eyes, she slipped out her smart phone and punched in a few numbers. Chase watched her without speaking, yet she felt something from him. Something dark, knowing and totally unexpected.

'What's your name?' he finally asked and, knowing she was being rude, she didn't look up from her phone.

'Millie Lang.' No work emails. Damn.

'What's that short for? Millicent? Mildred?'

She finally glanced up, saw him still studying her. 'Camilla.'

'Camilla,' he repeated, savouring the syllables, drawing them out with a sensual consideration that didn't seem forced or fake. 'I like it.' He gestured to her phone. 'So what's going on in the real world, Camilla? Your stock portfolio sound? Work managing without you?'

She flushed and put her phone away. She'd just been about to check NASDAQ. For the fifth time today. 'Everything ship-shape. And please don't call me Camilla.'

'You prefer Millie?'

'Clearly.'

He laughed. 'This is going to be a fun evening, I can tell.'

Her flush intensified, swept down her body. What a mistake this was—a stupid, stupid mistake. Had she actually thought she could do this—have dinner, have fun, *flirt*? All ridiculous.

'Maybe I should just go.' She half-rose from her chair, but Chase stopped her with one hand on her wrist. The touch of his fingers, long, lean and cool against that tender skin, felt like a bomb going off inside her body. Not just the usual tingle of attraction, the shower of sparks that was your body's basic reaction to a good-looking guy. No, a *bomb*. She jerked her hand away, heard her breath come out in a rush. 'Don't—'

'Whoa.' He held his hands up in front of him. 'Sorry, my mistake.' But he didn't look sorry. He looked like he knew exactly what she'd just experienced. 'I meant what I said, Millie. It's going to be a fun evening. I like a challenge.'

'Oh, please.' His stupid comment made her feel safe. She wanted this Chase to be exactly what she'd thought he was: attractive, arrogant and utterly unthreatening.

Chase grinned. 'I knew you'd expect me to say that.' And, just like that, she was back to wondering. Millie snatched up a menu.

'Shall we order?'

'Drinks first.'

'I'll have a glass of Chardonnay with ice, please.'

'That sounds about right,' he murmured and rose from

the table. Millie watched him walk to the bar, her gaze glued to his easy, long-limbed stride. Yes, she was staring at his butt. He looked good in board shorts.

By sheer force of will she dragged her gaze away from him and stared down at her phone. Why couldn't she have one work crisis? She'd had a dozen a day when she was in the office. Of course she knew why; she just didn't like it. Jack had insisted she take a week's holiday with no interruptions or furtive tele-commuting. She hadn't taken any in two years, and new company policy—supposedly for the health of its employees—demanded that you use at least half of your paid leave in one year.

What a ridiculous policy.

She *wanted* to work. She'd been working twelve-, fourteen- and sometimes even sixteen-hour days for two years and screeching to a halt to come here was making her very, very twitchy.

'Here you go.' Chase had returned to the table and placed a glass of wine in front of her. Millie eyed his own drink warily; it looked like soda.

'What are you drinking?'

'Some kind of cola.' He shrugged. 'It's cold, at least.'

'Do you have a drinking problem?' she asked abruptly and he laughed.

'Good idea, let's skip right to the important stuff. No, I don't. I'm just not drinking right now.' He took a sip of his soda, eyeing her thoughtfully. Millie held his gaze. All right, asking that had been a bit abrupt and even weird, but she'd forgotten how to do chit-chat.

'So, Millie, where are you from?'

'New York City.'

'I suppose I should have guessed that.'

'Oh, really?' She bristled. Again. 'You seem to think you have me figured out.'

'No, but I tend to be observant. And you definitely have that hard city gloss.'

'Where are you from, then?'

He gave her one of his toe-curling smiles. His eyes, Millie thought distantly, were so warm. She wanted to curl up in them, which was a nonsensical thought. 'I'm from New York too.'

'I suppose I could have guessed that.'

He laughed, a low, rich chuckle. 'How?'

'You've got that over-privileged, city-boy veneer,' she responded sweetly, to which he winced with theatrical exaggeration.

'Ouch.'

'At least now we understand each other.'

'Do we?' he asked softly and Millie focused on her drink. *Sip. Stare at the ice cubes bobbing in the liquid. Don't look at him.* 'Why are you so prickly?'

'I'm not.' It was a knee-jerk response. She *was* being prickly. She hadn't engaged with a man in any sense in far too long and she didn't know how to start now. *Why* had she agreed to this? She took another sip of wine, let the bubbles crisp on her tongue. 'Sorry,' she said after a moment. 'I'm not usually quite this bitchy.'

'I bring out the best in you?'

'I suppose you do.' She met his gaze, meaning to smile with self-deprecating wryness, but somehow her lips froze in something more like a grimace. He was gazing at her with a sudden intentness that made her breath dry and her heart start to pound. She wanted him to be light, wry, *shallow*. He wasn't being any of those things right now. And, even when he had been, she had a horrible feeling he'd simply done it by choice.

'So why are you on St Julian's?' he asked.

'Holiday, of course.'

'You don't seem like the type to holiday willingly.'

Which was all too true, but she didn't like him knowing it, or knowing anything. 'Oh?' she asked, glad to hear she was hitting that self-deprecating note she'd tried for earlier. 'And you know me so well?'

He leaned forward, suddenly predatory. 'I think I do.'

Her heart still pounding, Millie leaned back as if she actually felt relaxed and arched an eyebrow. 'How is that?'

'Let's see.' He leaned back too, sprawled in his chair in a manner so casually relaxed and yet also innately powerful, even in an ocean-side bar wearing board shorts. 'You're a lawyer, or else you're in finance.' He glanced at her, considering, and Millie froze. 'Finance, I'd say, something demanding but also elite. Hedge-fund manager, maybe?'

Damn it. How the hell did he know that? She said nothing.

'You work long hours, of course,' Chase continued, clearly warming to this little game. 'And you live in a high-rise building, full-service, on— Let's see. The Upper East Side? But near the subway, so you can get to work in under twenty minutes. Although you try to jog to work at least two mornings a week.' Now he arched an eyebrow, a little smile playing about his mouth. 'How am I doing so far?'

'Terrible,' Millie informed him shortly. She was seething inside, seething with the pain of someone knowing her at all, even just the basics. And she hated that he'd been able to guess it, read her as easily as a book. What else could he find out about her just by his so-called powers of observation? 'I run to work three mornings a week, not two, and I live in midtown.'

Chase grinned. 'I must be slipping.'

'Anyway,' Millie said, 'I could guess the same kinds of things about you.'

'OK, shoot.'

She eyed him just as he had her, trying to gain a little

time to assemble her thoughts. She had no idea what he did or where he lived. She could guess, but that was all it would be—a guess. Taking a breath, she began. 'I think you work in some pseudo-creative field, like IT or advertising.'

'*Pseudo*-creative?' Chase interjected, nearly spluttering his soda. 'You really are tough, Camilla.'

'Millie,' she reminded him shortly. Only Rob had called her Camilla. 'You live in Chelsea or Soho, in one of those deluxe bachelor loft apartments. A converted warehouse with views of the river and zero charm.'

'That is so stereotypical, it hurts.'

'With a great room that's fantastic for parties, top-of-the-line leather sofas, a huge TV and a high-tech kitchen full of gadgets you never use.'

He shook his head slowly, his gaze fastened on hers. He smiled, almost looking sorry for her. 'Totally wrong.'

She folded her arms. Strange how her observations of him made her feel exposed. 'Oh? How so?'

'All right, you might be right about the loft apartment, but it's in Tribeca—and my television is mid-size, thank you very much.'

'And the leather sofas?'

'Leather cleans very easily, or so my cleaning lady tells me.' She rolled her eyes. 'And I'll have you know I do use my kitchen, quite often. I find cooking relaxing.'

She eyed him uncertainly. 'You do not.'

'I do. But I bet you don't cook. You buy a bagel on the way to work, skip lunch and eat a bowl of cereal standing by the sink for dinner.'

It was just a little too close to the truth and it sounded unbelievably pathetic. Suddenly Millie wanted to stop this little game. Desperately. 'I order take-out on occasion as well,' she told him, trying for breezy. 'So what do you do, anyway?'

'I'm an architect. Does that count as pseudo-creative?'

'Definitely.' She was being incredibly harsh, but she was afraid to be anything else. This man exposed her in a way that felt like peeling back her skin—painful and messy. This date was over.

'As entertaining as this has been, I think I'll go.' She drained her glass of wine and half-rose from her chair, only to be stopped by Chase wrapping his fingers around her wrist, just as he had before—and, just as before, she reacted, an explosion of senses inside her.

'Scared, Millie?'

'Scared?' she repeated as contemptuously as she could. 'Of what—you?'

'Of us.'

'There is no *us*.'

'There's been an *us* since the moment you agreed to a drink, dinner and a walk on the beach,' he informed her with silky softness. 'And so far we've just had our drink.'

'Let me go,' she said flatly, her lips numb, her whole body buzzing.

Chase held up both hands, his gaze still holding hers as if they were joined by a live wire. 'I already did.'

And so he had. She was standing there like a complete idiot, acting as if she were trapped, when the only thing imprisoning her was her own fear. This man guessed way too much.

She couldn't walk away now. Admitting defeat was not an option. And if she could handle this, handle him as she'd assured herself she could, then wouldn't that be saying something? Wouldn't that be a way of proving to herself, as well as him, that she had nothing either to hide or fear?

She dropped back down into her chair and gave him a quick, cool smile. 'I'm not scared.'

Something like approval lit his eyes, making Millie feel

stupidly, ridiculously gratified. Better to get through this evening as quickly as possible.

'So shall we order?'

'Oh no, we're not eating here,' Chase informed her. Millie stared at him, nonplussed. He smiled, slow, easy and completely in control. 'We'll eat somewhere more private.'

CHAPTER TWO

'MORE private?' Millie's voice rose in a screech as she stared at him, two angry blotches of colour appearing high on her cheeks. He should be annoyed by now, Chase mused. He should be way past annoyed. The woman was a nutcase. Or at least very high-maintenance. But he wasn't annoyed, not remotely. He'd enjoyed their little exchange, liked that she gave as good as she got. And he was intrigued by something underneath that hard gloss—something real and deep and alive. He just wasn't sure what it was, or what he wanted to do with it.

But first, dinner. 'Relax. I'm not about to about to abduct you, as interesting as that possibility may be.'

'Not funny.'

She held herself completely rigid, her face still flushed with anger. He'd had no idea his change of dinner plans would provoke such a reaction—no; he had. Of course he had. He just hadn't realised he'd enjoy it so much. Underneath the overly ironed blouse her chest rose and fell in agitated breaths, making him suspect all that creaseless cotton hid some slender but interesting curves. 'You're right, it's not funny,' he agreed with as much genuine contrition as he could muster. 'We barely know each other, and I didn't intend to make you feel vulnerable.'

She rolled her eyes. 'We're not on some mandatory course

for creating a safe work environment, Chase. You can skip the PC double-speak.'

He laughed, loving it. Loving that she didn't play games, not even innocent ones. 'OK. Fine. By more private, I meant a room in the resort. Chaperoned by wait staff and totally safe. If you're feeling, you know, threatened.'

'I have not felt threatened by you for an instant,' Millie replied, and Chase leaned forward.

'Are you sure about that?' he asked softly, knowing he was pressing her in ways she didn't want to be pressed. He'd seen that shadow of vulnerability in her eyes, felt the sudden, chilly withdrawal as her armour went up. He knew the tactics because he'd used them himself.

It's not good news, Chase. I'm sorry.

Hell, yeah, he'd used them.

She stared at him for a moment, held his gaze long enough so he could see the warm brown of her eyes. Yes, *warm*. Like dark honey or rum, and the only warm thing about her. So far.

'Threatened is the wrong word,' she finally said, and from the starkness of her tone he knew she was speaking in total truth. 'You do make me uncomfortable, though.'

'Do I?'

She gave him a thin-lipped smile. 'I don't think anyone likes being told that it's obvious she eats a bowl of cereal by the sink for dinner.'

Ouch. Put like that, he realised it was insulting. 'I wouldn't say obvious.' Although he sort of would.

'Only because you're so perceptive, I suppose?' she shot back, and he grinned.

'So shall we go somewhere more private so you can continue to be uncomfortable?'

'What an appealing proposition.'

'It appeals to me,' he said truthfully, and she gave a little shake of her head.

'Honestly? What do you see in me?' She sounded curious, but also that thing he dreaded: vulnerable. She really didn't know the answer, and hell if he did either.

'What do you see in me?' he asked back.

She chewed her lip, her eyes shadowing once more. 'You made me laugh for the first time in—a long time.'

He had the strange feeling she'd been about to give him a specific number. *Since when?* 'That's a lot of pressure.'

Her eyes widened, flaring with warmth again. 'Why?'

'Because of course now I have to make you laugh again.'

And for a second he thought he might get a laugh right then and there, and something rose in his chest, an airy bubble of hope and happiness that made absolutely no sense. Still he felt it, rising him high and dizzily higher even though he didn't move. He grinned. Again, simply because he couldn't help it.

She shook her head. 'I'm not that easy.'

'This conversation just took a *very* interesting turn.'

'I meant *laughing*,' she protested, and then she did laugh, one ridiculously un-ladylike hiccup of joy that had her clapping her hand over her mouth.

'There it is,' Chase said softly. He felt a deep and strangely primal satisfaction, the kind he usually only felt when he'd nailed an architectural design. He'd made her laugh. Twice.

She stared at him, her hand still clapped over her mouth, her eyes wide, warm and soft—if eyes could even be considered soft. Chase felt a stirring deep inside—low down, yes, he felt that basic attraction, but something else. Something not quite so low down and far more alarming, caused by this hard woman with the soft eyes.

'You changed the deal,' she told him, dropping her hand,

all businesslike and brisk again. 'You said dinner here, in the restaurant.'

'I did not,' Chase countered swiftly. 'You just didn't read the fine print.'

He thought she might laugh again, but she didn't. He had a feeling she suppressed it, didn't want to give him the power of making her laugh three times. And it did feel like power, heady and addictive. He wanted more.

'I don't remember signing,' she said. 'And verbal agreements aren't legally binding.'

He leaned back in his chair, amazed at how alive he felt. How invigorated. He hadn't felt this kind of dazzling, creative energy in months. Eight months and six days, to be precise.

'All right, then,' he said. 'You can go.' He felt his heart thud at the thought that she might actually rise from the table and walk down the beach out of his life. Yet he also knew he had to level the playing field. She needed to be here because she wanted to be here, and she had to admit it. He didn't know why it was so important; he just felt it—that gut instinct that told him something was going on here that was more than a meal.

She chewed her lip again and he could tell by the little worry marks in its lush fullness—her lips were another soft part of her—that this was a habit. Her lashes swept downwards, hiding her eyes, but he could still read her. Easily.

She wanted to walk, but she also didn't, and that was aggravating her to no end.

She looked up, eyes clear and wide once more, any emotion safely hidden. 'Fine. We'll go somewhere more private.' And, without waiting for him, she rose from the table.

Chase rose too, anticipation firing through him. He wasn't even sure what he was looking forward to—just being with her, or something else? She was so not his type, and yet he

couldn't deny that deep jolt of awareness, the flash of lust.
And not just a flash, not just lust either. She attracted and
intrigued him on too many levels.

Smiling, he rose from the table and led the way out of the
beach-side bar and towards the resort.

Millie followed Chase into the resort, the soaring space cool
and dim compared to the beach. She felt neither cool nor dim;
everything inside her was light and heat. It scared her, feeling this. Wanting him. Because, yes, she knew she wanted
him. Not just desire, simple attraction, a biological response
or scientific law. *Want*.

She hadn't touched a man in two years. Longer, really,
because she couldn't actually remember the last time she
and Rob had made love. It had bothered her at first, the
not knowing. She'd lain in bed night after endless nights
scouring her brain for a fragment of a memory. Something
to remind her of how she'd lain sated and happy in her husband's arms. She hadn't come up with anything, because it
had been too long.

Now it wasn't the past that was holding her in thrall; it
was the present. The future. Just what did she want to happen tonight?

'This way,' Chase murmured, and Millie followed him
into a lift. The space was big enough, all wood-panelled luxury, but it still felt airless and small. He was still only wearing board shorts. Was he going to spend the whole evening
shirtless? Could she stand it?

Millie cleared her throat, the sound seeming as loud as a
gunshot, and Chase gave her a lazy sideways smile. He knew
what she was thinking. Feeling. Knew, with that awful arro-
gance, that she was attracted to him even if she didn't like it.
And she didn't like it, although she couldn't really say why.

It had been two years. Surely it was time to move on, to accept and heal and go forward?

She shook her head, impatient with herself. Dinner with someone like Chase was not going forward. If anything, it was going backwards, because he was too much like Rob. He was, Millie thought, more like Rob than Rob himself. He was her husband as her husband had always wanted to be: powerful, rich, commanding. He was Rob on steroids.

Exactly what she didn't want.

'Slow down there, Millie.'

Her gaze snapped to his, saw the remnant of that lazy smile. 'What—?'

'Your mind is going a mile a minute. I can practically see the smoke coming out of your ears.'

She frowned, wanting to deny it. 'It's just dinner.'

Chase said nothing, but his smile deepened. Millie felt a weird, shivery sensation straight through her bones that he wasn't responding because he didn't agree with her. It wasn't just dinner. It was something else, something scary.

But what?

'Here we are.' The lift doors swooshed open and Chase led her down a corridor and then out onto a terrace. A private terrace. They were completely alone, no wait staff in sight.

Millie didn't feel vulnerable, threatened or scared. No, she felt *terrified*. What was she doing here? Why had she agreed to dinner with this irritating and intriguing man? And why did she feel that jolt of electric awareness, that kick of excitement, every time she so much as looked at him? She felt more alive now than she had since Rob's death, maybe even since before that—a long time before that.

She walked slowly to the railing and laid one hand on the wrought-iron, still warm from the now-sinking sun. The vivid sunset had slipped into a twilit indigo, the sea a dark, tranquil mirror beneath.

'We missed the best part,' Chase murmured, coming to stand next to her.

'Do you think so?' Millie kept her gaze on the darkening sky. 'This part is more beautiful to me.'

Chase cocked his head, and Millie turned to see his speculative gaze slide over her. 'Somehow that doesn't surprise me,' he said, and reached out to tuck a strand of hair behind her ear. Millie felt as if he'd just dusted her with sparks, jabbed her with little jolts of electricity. Her cheek and ear throbbed, her physical response so intense it felt almost painful.

Did he feel it? Could it be possible that he reacted to her the way she did to him? The thought short-circuited her brain. It was quite literally mind-blowing.

She turned away from him, back to the sunset. 'Everybody likes the vibrant colours of a sunset,' she said, trying to keep her voice light. 'All that magenta and orange—gorgeous but gaudy, like an old broad with too much make-up.'

'I'll agree with you that the moment after is more your style. Understated elegance. Quiet sophistication.'

'And which do you prefer? The moment before or after?'

Chase didn't answer, and Millie felt as if the very air had suddenly become heavy with expectation. It filled her lungs, weighed them down; she was breathless.

'Before,' he finally said. 'Then there's always something to look forward to.'

Millie didn't think they were talking about sunsets any more. She glanced at Chase and saw him staring pensively at the sky, now deepening to black. The sun and all its gaudy traces had disappeared completely.

'So tell me,' she said, turning away from the railing, 'how did you arrange a private terrace so quickly? Or do you keep one reserved on standby, just in case you meet a woman?'

He laughed, a rich, throaty chuckle. This man enjoyed

life. It shouldn't surprise her; she'd labelled him a hedonist straight off. Yet she didn't feel prissily judgmental of that enjoyment right now. She felt—yes, she really did—*jealous*.

'Full disclosure?'

'Always.'

He reached for a blue button-down shirt that had been laid on one of the chairs. He'd thought of everything, and possessed the power to see it done. Millie watched him button up his shirt with long, lean fingers, the gloriously sculpted muscles of his chest disappearing under the crisp cotton.

'My family owns this resort.'

She jerked her rather admiring gaze from the vicinity of his chest to his face. 'Ah.' There was, she knew, a wealth of understanding in that single syllable. So, architect *and* trust-fund baby. She'd suspected something like that. He had the assurance that came only from growing up rich and entitled. She should be relieved; she wanted him to be what she'd thought he was, absolutely no more and maybe even less. So why, gazing at him now, did she feel the tiniest bit disappointed, like he'd let her down?

Like she actually wanted him to be different?

'Yes. Ah.' He smiled wryly, and she had a feeling he'd guessed her entire thought process, not for the first time this evening.

'That must be handy.'

'It has its benefits.' He spoke neutrally, without the usual flippant lightness and Millie felt a little dart of curiosity. For the first time Chase looked tense, his jaw a little bunched, his expression a little set. He didn't smile as he pulled out a chair for her at the cozy table for two and flickered with candlelight in the twilit darkness.

Millie's mind was, as usual, working overtime. 'The Bryant family owns this resort.'

'Bingo.'

'My company manages their assets.' That was how she'd ended up here, waiting out her week of enforced holiday, indolent luxury. Jack had suggested it.

'And you have a rule about mixing business with pleasure?'

'The point is moot. I don't handle their account.'

'Well, that's a relief.' He spoke with an edge she hadn't heard since she'd met him. Clearly his family and its wealth raised his hackles.

'So you're one of the Bryants,' she said, knowing instinctively such a remark would annoy him. 'Which one?'

'You know my family?'

'Who doesn't?' The Bryants littered the New York tabloids and society pages, not that she read either. But you couldn't so much as check your email without coming across a news blurb or scandalous headline. Had she read about Chase? Probably, if she'd paid attention to such things. There were three Bryant boys, as far as she remembered, and they were all players.

'I'm the youngest son,' Chase said tautly. He leaned back in his chair, deliberately relaxed in his body if not his voice. 'My older brother Aaron runs the property arm of Bryant Enterprises. My middle brother Luke runs the retail.'

'And you do your own thing.'

'Yes.'

That dart of curiosity sharpened into a direct stab. Why didn't Chase work for the family company? 'There's no Bryant Architecture, is there?'

His mouth thinned. 'Definitely not.'

'So what made you leave the family fold?'

'We're getting personal, then?'

'Are we?'

'Why did you throw out your canvas?'

Startled, she stared at him, saw his sly, silky little smile. 'I asked you first.'

'I don't like taking orders. And you?'

'I don't like painting.'

He stared at her; she stared back. A stand-off. So she wasn't the only one with secrets. 'Interesting,' he finally mused. He poured them both sparkling water. 'You don't like painting, but you decided to drag all that paraphernalia to the beach and set up your little artist's studio right there on the sand?'

She shrugged. 'I used to like it, when I was younger.' A lot younger and definitely less jaded. 'I thought I might like to try it again.'

'What changed your mind?'

Another shrug. She could talk about this. This didn't have to be personal or revealing. She wouldn't let it be. 'I just wasn't feeling it.'

'You don't seem like the type to rely on feelings.'

She smiled thinly. 'Still typecasting me, Chase?'

He laughed, an admitted defeat. 'Sorry.'

'It's OK. I play to type.'

'On purpose.'

She eyed him uneasily. Perhaps this was personal after all. And definitely revealing. 'Maybe.'

'Which means you aren't what you seem,' Chase said softly, 'are you?'

'I'm exactly what I seem.' She sounded defensive. *Great.*

'You *want* to be exactly what you seem,' he clarified. 'Which is why you play it that way.'

She felt a lick of anger, which was better than the dizzying combination of terror and lust he'd been stirring up inside her. 'What did you do, dust off your psychology textbook?'

He laughed and held up his hands. 'Guilty. I'm bored on this holiday, what can I say?'

And, just like that, he'd defused the tension that had been thickening in the air, tightening inside her. Yet Millie could not escape the feeling—the certainty—that he'd chosen to do it, that he'd backed off because he'd wanted to, not because of what she wanted.

One person at this table was calling the shots and it wasn't her.

'So.' She breathed through her nose, trying to hide the fact that her heart was beating hard. She wanted to take a big, dizzying gulp of air, but she didn't. Wouldn't. 'If you're so bored, why are you on holiday?'

'Doctor's orders.'

She blinked, not sure if he was joking. 'How's that?'

'The stress was getting to me.'

He didn't look stressed. He looked infuriatingly relaxed, arrogantly in control. 'The holiday must be working.'

'Seems to be.' He sounded insouciant, yet deliberately so. He was hiding something, Millie thought. She'd tried to strike that note of breeziness too many times not to recognise its falseness.

'So are we actually going to eat?' He hadn't pressed her, so she wouldn't press him. Another deal, this one silently made.

'Your wish is my command.'

Within seconds a waiter appeared at the table with a tray of food. Millie watched as he ladled freshly grilled snapper in lime juice and coconut rice on her plate. It smelled heavenly.

She waited until he'd served Chase and departed once more before saying dryly, 'Nice service. Being one of the Bryant boys has its perks, it seems.'

'Sometimes.' Again that even tone.

'Are you staying at the resort?'

'I have my own villa.' He stressed the 'own' only a little, but Millie guessed it was a sore point. Had he worked for what he had? He was probably too proud to tell her. She wouldn't ask.

She took a bite of her fish. It tasted heavenly too, an explosion of tart and tender on her tongue. She swallowed and saw Chase looking at her. Just looking, no deliberate, heavy-lidded languor, and yet she felt her body respond, like an antenna tuned to some cerebral frequency. Everything jumped to alert, came alive.

It had been so *long*.

She took another bite.

'So why are you on holiday, Millie?'

Why did the way he said her name sound intimate? She swallowed the fish. 'Doctor's orders.'

'Really?'

'Well, no. Boss's. I haven't taken any holiday in a while.'

'How long?'

That bite of fish seemed to lodge in her chest, its exquisite tenderness now as tough as old leather. Finally, with an audible and embarrassing gulp, she managed, 'Two years.'

Chase cocked his head and continued just looking. How much did he *see*? 'That's a long time,' he finally said, and she nodded.

'So he told me.'

'But you didn't want to take any holiday?'

'It's obvious, I suppose.'

'Pretty much.'

She stabbed a bit of rice with her fork. 'I like to work.'

'So *are* you a hedge-fund manager?'

'Got it in one.'

'And you like it?'

Instinctively '*of course I do*' rose to her lips, yet somehow the words didn't come. She couldn't get them out, as if someone had pressed a hand over her mouth and kept her from speaking. So she just stared and swallowed and felt herself flush.

Why had he even asked? she wondered irritably. Obviously she liked it, since she worked so hard.

'I see,' Chase said quietly, knowingly, and a sudden, blinding fury rose up in her, obliterating any remaining sense and opening her mouth.

'You don't see anything.' She sounded savage. Incensed. And, even worse, she *was*. Why did this stupid man make her feel so much? Reveal so much?

'Maybe not,' Chase agreed. He didn't sound riled in the least. Millie let out a shuddering breath. This date had been such a bad idea.

'OK, now it's your turn.'

She blinked. 'What?'

'You get to ask me a personal question. Only fair, right?'

Another blink. She hadn't expected that. 'Why do you hate being one of the Bryants?'

Now he blinked. 'Hate is a strong word.'

'So it is.'

'I never said I hated it.'

'You didn't need to.' She took a sip of water, her hand steady, her breath thankfully even. 'You're not the only one who can read people, you know.'

'You can read me?' Chase leaned forward, his eyes glinting in the candlelight. She saw the golden-brown stubble on his jaw, could almost feel its sandpaper roughness under her fingers. She breathed in the scent of him, part musk, part sun, pure male. 'What am I thinking now?' he asked, a steely, softly worded challenge. Millie didn't dare answer.

She knew what she was thinking. She was thinking about taking that hard jaw between her hands and angling her lips over his. His lips would be soft but firm, commanding and drawing deep from her. And she would give, she would surrender that long-held part of herself in just one kiss. She knew it, felt it bone-deep, soul-deep, which was ridiculous, because she barely knew this man. Yet in the space of an hour or two he'd drawn more from her than anyone had since her husband's death, or even before. He'd seen more, glimpsed her sadness and subterfuge like no one else could or had. Not even the parents who adored her, the sister she called a best friend. No one had seen through her smoke and mirrors. No one but Chase.

And he was a *stranger*.

A stranger who could kiss her quite senseless.

'I don't know what you're thinking,' she said and looked away.

Chase laughed softly, no more than an exhalation of breath. 'Coward.'

And yes, maybe she was a coward, but then he was too. Because Millie knew the only reason Chase had turned pro-vocative on her was because he didn't want to answer her question about his family.

She pushed her plate away, her appetite gone even though her meal was only half-finished. 'How about that walk on the beach?'

He arched an eyebrow. 'You're done?'

She was *so* done. The sooner she ended this evening, the better. The only reason she wasn't bailing on the walk was her pride. Even now, when she felt uncomfortable, exposed and even angry, she was determined to handle this. Handle him. 'It was delicious,' she said. 'But I've had enough.'

'No pun intended, I'm sure.'

She curved her lips into a smile. 'You can read into that whatever you like.'

'All right, Millie,' Chase said, uncoiling from his chair like a lazy serpent about to strike. 'Let's walk.'

He reached for her hand and unthinkingly, *stupidly*, Millie let him take it.

As soon as his fingers wrapped over hers, she felt that explosion inside her again and she knew she was lost.

CHAPTER THREE

CHASE felt Millie's fingers tense in his even as a buzz travelled all the way up his arm. Her fingers felt fragile, slender bone encased in tender skin. A sudden need to protect her rose in him, a caveman's howl. Clearly it was some kind of evolutionary instinct, because if there was one woman who didn't need protecting, it was Camilla Lang.

He thought she might jerk her hand away from his, and he was pretty sure she wanted to, but she didn't. Didn't want to show weakness, most likely. He smiled and took full advantage, tightening his hold, drawing her close. She tensed some more.

This woman was *prickly*. And Chase had a sneaking suspicion she had issues, definitely with a capital I. Bad relationship or broken heart; maybe something darker and more difficult. Who knew? He sure as hell didn't want to. Didn't he have enough to deal with, with his own issues? Those had a capital I too. And he had no intention of sharing them with Millie.

Even so he drew her from the table, still holding her hand, and away from the terrace, down the lift, through the resort, all the way outside. He threaded his way through the tables of the beach-side restaurant and bar, straight onto the sand. She held his hand the whole time, not speaking, not pulling away, but clearly not all that pleased about it either.

There they were, holding hands alone in the dark.

The wind rattled the leaves of the palm trees overhead and he could hear the gentle *shoosh* of the waves lapping against the shore. The resort and its patrons seemed far away, their voices barely a murmur, the night soft and dark all around them. Millie pulled her hand from his, a not-so-gentle tug.

'Let's walk.'

'Sounds good.'

Silently they walked down the beach, the sand silky and cool under their bare feet. Lights of a pleasure yacht glimmered in the distance, and from far away Chase heard the husky laugh of a woman intent on being seduced.

Not like Millie. She walked next to him, her back ramrod-straight, her capris and blouse still relentlessly unwrinkled. She looked like she was walking the plank.

He nearly stopped right there in the sand. What the *hell* was he doing here, with a woman like her? Didn't he have better ways to spend his time?

'What?' She turned to him, and in the glimmer of moonlight he saw those warm, soft eyes, shadowed with a vulnerability he knew she thought she was hiding.

'What do you mean, *what*?'

'You're thinking something.'

'I'm always thinking something. Most people are.'

She shook her head, shadows deepening in her eyes. 'No, I mean…' She paused, biting her lip, teeth digging into those worry marks once more. If she didn't let up, she'd have a scar. 'You're regretting this, aren't you? This whole stupid date.'

He stopped, faced her full-on. 'Aren't you?'

She let go of her lip to give him the smallest of smiles. 'That's a given, don't you think?'

Did it have to be? How had they fallen into these roles so quickly, so easily? He wanted to break free. He didn't want to be a flippant playboy to her uptight workaholic. He had a sudden, mad urge to push her down into the sand, to see her clothes wrinkled and dirty, her face smudged and sandy, her lips swollen and kissed...

Good grief.

Chase took a step back, raking a hand through his hair. 'We're pretty different, Millie.'

'Thank God for that.'

He couldn't muster a laugh. He had too many emotions inside him: longing and lust, irritation and irrational fear. What an unholy mix. He'd asked her out because it had seemed fun, *amusing*, but it was starting to feel way too intense. And he didn't need any more intense. He took a breath and let it out slowly. 'Maybe we should call it a night.'

She blinked, her face immediately blanking, as if her mind were pressing delete. Inwardly Chase cursed. He didn't want to hurt her, but he knew in that moment he had.

'Millie—'

'Fine.' Her back straighter than ever, she started down the beach away from the resort. He watched her for a second, exasperated with her stubbornness and annoyed by his own clumsy handling of the situation.

'Aren't you staying at the resort?'

'I'm finishing our walk.'

He let out a huff of laughter. He *liked* this woman, issues and all. 'I didn't realise we'd set a distance on it.'

'More than ten seconds.' She didn't look back once.

She was far enough away that he had to shout. 'It was more like five minutes.'

'Clearly you have very little stamina.'

There was more truth in that then he'd ever care to admit. 'Millie.' He didn't shout this time, but he knew she heard anyway. He saw it in the tensing of her shoulders, the half-second stumble in her stride. 'Come back here.'

'Why should I?'

'On second thought, I'll come to you.' Quickly he strode down the beach, leaving deep footprints in the damp sand, until he reached her. The wind had mussed her hair just a little bit, so the razor edges were softened, blurred. Without even thinking what he was doing or wondering if it was a good idea, Chase reached out and slid his hands along her jaw bone, cupping her face as he drew her to him. Her skin felt like cool silk, cold silk, icy even. Yet so very, unbearably soft. Eyes and lips and skin, all soft. What about her, Chase wondered, was actually hard?

She was close enough to kiss, another inch would do it, yet he didn't. She didn't resist, didn't do anything. She was like a deer caught in the headlights, a rabbit in a snare. Trapped. Terrified.

'Sorry,' he breathed against her mouth, close enough so he could imagine the taste of her. She'd taste crisp and clean, like the white wine she'd drunk, except it would be just her. Essence of Camilla.

She jerked back a mere half-inch. 'Sorry for what?'

'For acting like a jerk.'

Her lips quirked in the tiniest of smiles. 'To which point of the evening are you referring?'

'All right, wise-ass. I was talking about two minutes ago, when I said we should call it a night.' He stroked his thumb over the fullness of her lower lip, because he just couldn't help himself, and felt her tremble. 'I don't think I was too much of a jerk before that.'

Millie didn't answer. Chase saw that her lips were parted, her pupils dilated. *Desire*. The brief moment of tenderness suddenly flared into something untamed and urgent. Chase felt a groan catch in his chest, his body harden in undeniable and instinctive response. His hands tightened as they cradled her face, yet neither of them moved. It was almost as if they were paralysed, both afraid—no, terrified—to close the mere inch that separated them, cross that chasm.

Because Chase knew it wouldn't be your average kiss. And he was in no position for anything else.

With one quick jerk of her head, Millie slid out of his grasp and stepped backwards. 'Thanks for the apology,' she said, her voice as cool as ever. 'But it's not needed. It was interesting to get to know you, Chase, but I think we've fulfilled both sides of the deal.' She smiled without humour, and Chase couldn't stand the sudden bleakness in her eyes. Damn it, they were meant to be *soft*. 'Good night,' she said and headed back down the beach.

Millie walked without looking where she was going or caring. She just wanted to get away from Chase.

What had just happened?

He'd almost kissed her. She'd almost let him. In that moment when his hands had slid along her skin, cradling her face like she was something to be cherished and treasured, she'd wanted him to. Desperately. She would have let him do anything then, and thank goodness he hadn't, thank God he'd hesitated and she'd somehow found the strength to pull away.

The last thing she needed was to get involved with a man like Chase Bryant.

She left the beach behind and wound her way through the palm trees to the other side of the resort. She'd go in the front entrance and up to her room, and with any luck she wouldn't see Chase again all week. It was a big place, and he'd told her he was staying at his villa.

So why did that thought fill her with not just disappointment, but desolation? It was ridiculous to feel so lost without a shallow stranger she'd met a couple of hours ago. Absolutely absurd.

Clearly what this evening had shown her, Millie decided

as she swiped her key-card and entered the sumptuous suite Jack had insisted she book for the week, was that she was ready to move on. Start dating, have some kind of relationship.

Just not with a man like Chase Bryant.

The words echoed through her, making her pause in stripping off her clothes and turning on the shower. *A man like Chase Bryant.* She'd pigeon-holed Chase from the moment she'd met him, yet he'd surprised her at every turn. Just what kind of man *was* he?

A man who asked pressing questions and told her things about herself nobody else knew. Who turned flippant just when she needed him to. Whose simple touch set off an explosion inside her, yet who kept himself from kissing her even when she was so clearly aching for his caress.

A man who made her very, very uncomfortable.

Was that the kind of man she didn't want to get involved with?

Hell, yes.

She wished she could dismiss him, as she'd fully intended to do when she'd first met him: spoiled and shallow playboy, completely non-threatening. That was the man she'd agreed to have dinner with, not the man he *was*, who had set her pulse racing and tangled her emotions into knots. A man who touched her on too many levels.

Was that what she didn't want? Getting involved with someone who had the power to see her as she really was, to hurt her?

Well, *duh*. Obviously she didn't want to get hurt. Who did? And surely she'd already had her life's share of grief Millie stepped into the shower, the water streaming over her even as her thoughts swirled in confusing circles.

Her mind was telling her all that, but her body was singing a very different tune. Her body wanted his touch. Her mouth wanted to know his kiss. Every bit of her ached with a longing for fulfilment she thought she'd forever suppressed.

She let out a shudder and leaned her head against the shower tile as the water streamed over her.

She could stay analytical about this. So she didn't want to get hurt. She didn't have to. How much she cared—how much she gave—was in her control. And here she was—and Chase was—on a tropical island for a single week, neither of them with very much to do...

Why not?

Why not what?

She dumped too much shampoo into the palm of her hand and scrubbed her hair, fingernails raking her scalp as if she could wash these tempting and terrible thoughts right out of her mind.

Just what was she contemplating?

A week-long affair with Chase Bryant. A fling. A cheap, sordid, sexual transaction.

She scrubbed harder.

She didn't do flings. Of course she didn't. Her husband had been her only lover. Yet here she was, thinking about it. Wondering how Chase would taste, how he would hold her. What it would feel like, to be in his arms. To surrender herself, just a little bit of herself, because even if he sensed she had secrets she wasn't going to tell them to him. She just wanted that physical release, that momentary connection. The opportunity to forget. When Chase had been about to kiss her, she hadn't been able to think about anything else. All thoughts and memories had fled, leaving her nothing but blissful sensation.

She wanted that again. *More*.

Millie rinsed off and turned off the shower. She could control this. She could satiate this hunger that had opened up inside her and prove to herself and everyone else that she'd moved on.

She just needed to tell Chase.

Chase watched the poker-straight figure march down the beach as if in step with an invisible army and wondered why on earth Millie was looking for him. For there could be no mistaking her intent; she'd arrowed in on him like a laser beam. What, he wondered, was with all the military references going through his mind?

Clearly Millie Lang was on the attack.

And he was quite enjoying the anticipation of an invasion. He sat back on his heels on the deck of his sailboat, the water lapping gently against its sides, the sun a balm on his back. Millie marched closer.

Chase had no idea what she wanted. He'd stopped trying to untangle his thoughts about their date last night, from the almost-kiss he hadn't acted on, to the hurt that had flashed in her eyes to the fact that it had taken him three hours to fall asleep, with Millie's soft eyes still dancing through his mind. Definitely better not to think about any of it.

'There you are.'

'Looking for me?'

She stood on the beach, feet planted in the sand, hands on hips, a look of resolute determination on her face. 'As a matter of fact, I am.'

'I'm intrigued.' He stood up, wincing a little at the ache in his joints. He couldn't ignore the pain any more. She watched him, eyes narrowed, and he smiled. He could ignore it. He would. 'So, what's on your mind, scary lady?'

Her mouth twitched in a suppressed smile, and then she was back to being serious. 'Is this your boat?'

He glanced back at the sailboat, doing an exaggerated double-take. 'What—this?'

'Very funny.'

'Yep, it's my boat.'

'Did you sail here?'

He laughed, reluctantly, because once he might have. Not any more. He didn't trust himself out on the sea alone. 'No, I flew in a plane like most people. I keep the boat moored here, though.'

'I suppose the Bryants are a big sailing family and you started at the yacht club when you were a baby.'

He heard an edge to her voice that he recognised. She hadn't grown up rich, suspected the proverbial silver spoon. 'More like a toddler,' he said, shrugging. 'Do you sail?'

Lips pressed together. 'No.'

'You should try it.'

She glanced at him suspiciously. 'Why?'

'Because it's fun. And freeing. And I'd like to see you out on the water, your hair blowing away from your face.' She'd look softer then, he thought. Happier too, maybe.

'You would, huh?'

'Yeah. I would.'

'Well, you already told me how you felt about my haircut.'

He chuckled. 'True. Feel free to let me know if there's anything you don't like about my appearance.'

She eyed him up and down deliberately, and Chase felt a lick of excitement low in his belly. He liked that slow, considering look. Millie Lang was checking him out. 'I will,' she said slowly, 'but there isn't anything yet.'

'No?' He felt it again, that licking flame firing him up inside. Was Millie *flirting*? What had changed since last night, when she'd been as sharp and jagged as a handful of splinters? When he'd let her walk away because he told himself it was better—or at least easier—that way.

And then hadn't stopped thinking about her all night.

'Come aboard,' he said, and stretched out a hand. She

eyed it warily, and then with a deep breath like she was about to go underwater she took it and clambered onto the boat.

It was a small sailboat, just thirty-two feet long with one cabin underneath. He'd bought it with his first bonus and sailed halfway around the world on it, back when he'd been a hotshot. Now he cruised in the shallows, like some seventy year old pensioner with a bad case of gout and a dodgy heart. No risks. No stress. No fun.

'It's…nice,' Millie said, and he knew she didn't know a thing about boats. Who cared? He liked seeing her on deck, even if her clothes were still way too wrinkle-free. Today she wore a red-and-white-striped top and crisp navy-blue capris. Very nautical. Very boring. Yet he was intrigued by the way the boat-neck of her top revealed the hard, angular line of her collarbone. He wanted to run his fingers along that ridge of bone, discover if her skin was as icily soft as it had been last night.

'I could take you out some time,' he said. 'On the boat.' Why was she here? He stepped closer to her, inhaled the scent of her, something clean and citrusy. Breathed deep.

She turned to him, her hair sweeping along her jaw, and his gaze was caught by the angles of her jaw and shoulder, hard and soft. Her top had slipped a little, and he could see the strap of her bra: beige lace. No sexy lingerie for this lady, yet he still felt himself go hard.

'You could,' she said slowly, and he knew she was gearing up to say something—but what?

He folded his arms, adopted a casual pose. 'So?'

'So what?'

'Why are you here, Millie?'

Again that trapped look, chin tilted with defiance. This woman was all contradiction. 'Do you mind?'

'Not a bit.' And that was the truth.

She turned away, rubbing her arms as if she were cold. 'How long are you on this island, anyway?'

'A week, give or take.'

'You're not sure?'

'I'm being flexible.'

'And then you go back to New York?'

'That's the plan.' This was starting to feel like an interrogation. He didn't mind, but he wondered what she was getting at.

'I've never come across you in New York,' she said, almost to herself, and Chase just about kept himself from rolling his eyes.

'It's a pretty big city.'

She turned to face him. 'And we move in completely different circles.'

'Seems like it.'

'So there's no chance we'd see each other again.'

Maybe he should start feeling offended. But he didn't; he just felt like smiling. Laughing. Why did he enjoy her prickliness so much? 'Is that what you're afraid of?'

She met his gaze squarely. 'I'd prefer it if we didn't.'

He rubbed his jaw. 'If that's what you'd prefer, why are you on my boat?'

'I meant after. After this week.' Her words seemed heavy with meaning, but he still didn't get it.

'OK. I think I can manage that.' Even if he wasn't sure he wanted to.

'It would be easier,' she said, sounding almost earnest now. 'For me.'

Now he was really confused. 'Millie, I have no idea what you're talking about.'

'I know.' She pressed her lips together, gave a decisive nod. OK, Chase thought, here it comes. 'I'm attracted to you. You probably know that.'

He lifted one shoulder in a shrug that could mean anything. He didn't want to ruin this moment by agreeing or disagreeing; he just wanted her to keep talking.

'And I think you're attracted to me. Sort of.'

She looked so pathetically and yet endearingly vulnerable that Chase had to keep himself from reaching for her. What he would do when he had her in his arms, he wasn't completely sure. He did know one thing. 'I'm attracted to you, Millie. More than I'd ever expect.'

She let out a short laugh. 'Because I'm not your usual type.'

'No, you're not. Does that matter?' He wasn't even sure what he was asking. Where was she going with this conversation?

'No, I don't think it does.' She didn't sound completely sure.

'But, trust me, I am.' If she risked a glance downwards, she'd know.

'Well. Good.'

'Glad we're on the same page.'

She let out a breath and looked straight in his eyes. Vulnerability and strength, hard and soft. 'I hope we are.'

'Maybe we'd find out if you clued me into where this conversation is going.'

'Fine.' She took a deep breath, plunged. 'I want to sleep with you.'

CHAPTER FOUR

To HIS credit, Chase's jaw didn't drop. He didn't laugh or raise his eyebrows or even blink. He just stared at her, expressionless, and Millie felt herself flush.

She'd decided on the straightforward approach because, really, what else could she do? She didn't flirt. She couldn't play the seductress, and in any case she knew instinctively that Chase would see through any gauzy ploys. No, all she had was a straight shot, and she'd fired it. Direct hit.

'OK,' Chase finally said, letting out a breath. 'That's… good to know.'

She gave a shaky huff of laughter. 'I'm glad you think so.'

He rubbed his jaw, the movement inherently sexy. She could see the rippling muscled six-pack of his abs, the glint of sun on his stubble, his strong arms and lean fingers. Yes, she was definitely attracted to him. 'So,' he said. 'What brought this about?'

Of course he'd start asking questions. Most guys would take what she said at face value and drop their pants. Not Chase. She should have realised this wasn't going to be simple.

She shifted her weight, tried to act at least somewhat nonchalant. 'What do you mean?'

'Why me?'

'You're here, you're interested and I'm attracted to you.'

He arched an eyebrow. 'I take it this isn't your normal behaviour?'

She swallowed, kept his stare. 'No, not exactly.'

'So why now?'

How much truth to tell? She decided to fire another straight shot. 'Look, I don't want to get into messy details. This isn't about emotion, or getting to know each other, or anything like that.'

'I appreciate your candour.'

'Good.' She felt that flush creep back. This had seemed like such a good idea last night, when she couldn't forget how much she'd wanted him to kiss her. When having a fling with Chase Bryant had seemed like the perfect way to move on from the spectres of her failed life. To forget, at least for a little while.

From here it wasn't looking so good.

'So?' she finally prompted, a definite edge to her voice.

'Well, I'm flattered.' Chase leaned over the boat to haul in some kind of rope. Millie waited, everything inside her tensing. He straightened, tossing the rope into a neat coil on the deck. 'But I'm not that easy a lay.'

She blinked, tried desperately to arrange her face into some sort of blankness. 'Oh? You could have fooled me.'

He looked almost amused. 'Now what gave you the impression that I was a man-whore, Miss Scary?'

'I didn't mean that.' Her face, Millie suspected, was bright red. 'I only meant you asked me out last night and so you must be…you know…open.'

'Open?' Now he really seemed amused.

'To a—a no-strings type of…' She trailed off, unwilling to put any of it in words. Affair? Fling? *Relationship?*

'Thing?' Chase supplied helpfully, and she nodded, bizarrely grateful.

'Yes. Thing.'

'Interesting.' He reached for another rope, and Millie felt the boat rock under her feet.

'So do you think you could give me your answer?' she asked, trying not to sound impatient. Or desperate.

'An answer,' Chase mused, and Millie gritted her teeth. He was tormenting her. On purpose.

'Yes, Chase. An answer.'

'As to whether I'll sleep with you.'

She heard the grinding screech as she gritted her teeth even harder. 'Yes.'

He smiled as he coiled another rope on the deck. 'The short answer is yes.'

She let out a quick, silent breath. 'And the long answer?'

'We'll do it on my terms.'

He turned to her, completely relaxed, utterly in control. Millie felt her heart flip over in her chest. It wasn't exactly a pleasant sensation. So, Chase would sleep with her. She would sleep with him. They would have sex.

Her body tingled. Her heart hammered and her mouth dried. Just what she had started here? And how would it finish?

'Relax, Millie. I'm not about to drop my pants.'

Even if that was what she'd wanted from him originally: a simple, quick, easy transaction. Now she didn't know what she wanted. She swallowed, tried to ease the dryness in her throat.

'So what are your terms?'

'Don't worry, I'll keep you informed as we go along.'

Too late Millie realised they were moving. They'd gone about twenty feet from the shore and Chase was doing something with the sails or rigging or whatever was on this wretched boat. She didn't know the first thing about sailing.

'What—what are you doing?' she demanded.

'Sailing.'

'But I don't—'

'I told you I wanted to see you on my boat,' Chase said with an easy smile. 'With your hair blowing away from your face.'

'But—'

'My terms, Millie.' His smile widened. Millie suppressed a short and violent curse. Just what had she got herself into? 'Relax,' he said. 'You could even enjoy yourself.'

'That *was* kind of the point,' she muttered, and he laughed. 'Glad to hear it.'

She watched Chase let out the sail, the white cloth snapping in the brisk breeze. They were quite far out from the shore now, far enough for Millie to feel a sudden pulse of alarm. She was alone on a boat in the middle—well, *sort* of the middle—of the Caribbean with a man. With Chase.

She didn't feel frightened, or even nervous. She felt... alert. Aware. *Alive*.

'OK,' she said, taking a step towards him. 'So where are we going?'

'Do we need a destination?'

'I'm kind of goal-oriented.'

'So I've noticed.'

Her hair was blowing in the breeze, but not away from her face. In it. Strands stuck to her lips and with an impatient sigh she brushed it away. Chase grinned in approval.

'There.'

'What?' she asked irritably. 'Is this some kind of weird fetish you have? Women and hair?'

'I just like seeing you look a bit more relaxed. More natural.' He paused, as if weighing his words. 'Soft.'

'Don't.' The single word came out sharp, a cut. 'Don't,' she said again, and this time it was a warning.

'What?'

'Don't—don't try to change me. This isn't about that.'

She couldn't stand it if he thought he was on some wretched mercy mission, making her relax and enjoy life. He had no idea. No clue whatsoever.

'What *is* it about?' Chase asked calmly. 'Sex?'

'Yes. I thought I made that clear.'

'You did.' Just as calmly he strode towards the sail and started doing something with it. Millie couldn't tell what. 'And I made it clear this would be on my terms. Watch out.'

'What—?'

She saw something heavy and wooden swing straight towards her face and then Chase's hands were on her shoulders, pulling her out of the way. She collided with his chest, her back coming against that bare, hard muscle. Her heart thudded and his hands felt hot on her shoulders, his thumbs touching the bare skin near her collarbone.

'What was that?' she asked shakily.

'The boom. I had to tack.'

'Tack?'

'Change direction. I should have warned you, but all this sex talk was distracting me.'

She had no answer to that. All she could think about was how warm and heavy his hands felt on her shoulders, how he'd only have to move his thumbs an inch or two to brush the tops of her breasts. How she wanted him to.

'We're good now,' he said, dropping his hands. 'We should have a pretty nice run. Let's sit down.'

Numbly Millie followed him to a cushioned bench in the back of the boat. Chase reached into a cooler and took out a bottle of sparkling water, offering it to her before he took one himself.

'Cheers. Sorry I don't have champagne to toast this momentous occasion.'

'So why don't you drink, exactly?'

'More doctor's orders. Reduce stress.' He spoke with that

deliberate lightness again. He wasn't telling her the truth, or at least not the whole truth.

Millie swallowed and took a sip of water. Her thoughts were racing as fast as the boat that skimmed lightly over the aquamarine sea onto an unknown horizon. *What was going to happen here?*

'So. Tell me more about these terms of yours.'

'The first one is I decide when we do the deed. And where. And how.'

She swallowed. 'That's asking for a lot of control.'

'I know. And I'm not asking. I'm telling.'

The bottle felt slippery in her hands. 'I'm not really comfortable with that.'

'OK.' He shrugged, everything so easy.

'What do you mean, OK?'

'The deal's off, then. No sex.'

She bit her lip. 'I didn't mean that.'

Another shrug. 'You want to sleep with me, you agree to my terms.'

'You make it sound so—cold.'

'No, Scary, you're doing that all on your own. You're the one who wants to have some hurried grope and then brush yourself off and move on with life.'

'I never said that.'

'Am I wrong?'

She looked away. 'It wouldn't have to be *hurried*.'

'What is this, some milestone? First time you'll have had sex since you broke up with your long-time boyfriend?'

She kept her gaze on the sea, frills of white amidst the endless blue. 'No.'

'Divorce?'

'No.'

He sighed. 'Something, though, right?'

'Maybe.'

'Fine. You don't want to tell me. No messy details.'

'That's right.'

'But I'm telling you I'm not interested in some soulless, sordid transaction. If you want that, hire an escort service. Or go hang out in the bar for a little while longer. Someone will pay or play.'

She blinked and set her jaw. 'As tempting as that sounds, I'm not interested.'

'Why not?'

'Because—' She hesitated. She felt as if he were stripping away her defences, and yet she didn't know how he was doing it. She kept darting around to cover her bases, but they were already gone. 'Because I don't want that.'

He leaned forward, his voice a soft, seductive whisper. 'What do you want, Millie?'

Reluctantly, she dragged her gaze towards him. His eyes glittered gold and the wind ruffled his hair. He looked completely gorgeous and so utterly sure. 'I want you.'

He held her gaze, triumph blazing in his eyes, a smile curving his mouth. *Damn it*. Why had she said that? Admitted so much?

'And I want you,' he told her in a low, lazy murmur. 'Rather a lot. But I want to be more than a milestone, and so we're doing this my way.'

More than a milestone. Already she was in over her head. She'd been so stupid, convincing herself that she could handle Chase, that he'd agree to some one-night stand. On the surface, he should have. But from the moment she'd met him he'd never been what she'd thought he was. What she wanted him to be.

So why had she pursued this? Why was she still here, still wanting to do this deal? Did she really want him that much?

Yes.

'Fine. We'll do it your way. But I want to know what that is first.'

His smile turned to a pie-eating grin. 'Nope.'

'Nope?'

'Nope. Information is given on a need-to-know basis only.'

Her fingers tightened on her bottle of water, her knuckles aching. 'I need to know, Chase.'

'I'll decide that.'

She could not believe how horribly autocratic and arrogant he was being. She could not believe she was taking it. Why on earth was she not telling him to piss off and take her back to the shore? Was there some sick, depraved little girl inside her who wanted to be told what to do?

Or did she just want him that much?

Yes, she did.

'Fine,' she said, forming the word through stiff lips. He nodded, no more. She took a sip of water to ease the dryness in her throat. 'So what now?' she asked once she'd swallowed and felt able to speak again.

'You take off your clothes.'

Her bottle of water slipped from her nerveless fingers and Chase reached forward to catch it.

'Easy there, Scary. I was joking. Right now we relax, enjoy the sun and sea. I'll let you know when clothes or lack thereof come into the equation.'

She shook her head slowly. 'Why are you doing this?'

'Doing what?'

'Toying with me.'

He arched an eyebrow. 'Is that what it feels like?'

'Pretty much.'

He didn't answer for a moment, just took a long swallow of water so she could see the brown column of his throat, the breadth of his chest tapering down to lean hips. He was beautiful. 'Well,' he finally said, his gaze meeting hers with too much knowledge, 'I suppose it's because you've been trying to toy with me.'

She took a startled step back. 'I have not.'

'Oh, really? You march over to my boat and practically demand to sleep with me. You think I'm just going to lie down and let you have your wicked way with me?'

'No…not exactly.'

'You think you can tell me how, when and where I'm going to have sex with you?'

'That's what you're trying to do with me!'

'Exactly. And I'm not going to be entered into your smart phone and then deleted when you're done. I'm not a hedge fund, Millie. I'm not an account or a client or a to-do item to tick off. And, more importantly, neither is what's between us.'

She felt as if he'd wrapped an iron band around her chest and *squeezed*. Breathing hurt. 'There's nothing between us.'

'That is bull and you know it.'

'What do you *want*, Chase?'

'You. Just like you want me. But I think we have very different definitions of just what that means.'

She dragged a breath into her constricted lungs. Spots danced before her eyes. She was in way over her head now; she was drowning and she had no idea how to save herself. 'I think we must,' she finally managed, and Chase just grinned.

Chase watched Millie process what he said and wondered if she was going to pass out. She'd gone seriously pale. And admittedly he'd laid it on pretty thick. He didn't even know why he was pushing so hard. He'd thought last night had been too intense, and yet today he'd upped the ante a hundred fold. He'd acted on instinct, telling her he was going to call the shots, not just because he didn't want to be her toy-boy but because he knew on a gut level she needed to let go of that precious control. And he wanted to be the one to make it happen.

As for what was *between* them... She was right. There was nothing between them, not really.

Yet.

So what did he want?

He took another long swallow of water, desperate for a cold beer. A distraction. He was scaring himself with all this talk. Asking for more than he'd ever intended to want, never mind have.

Maybe he was acting this way because ever since his diagnosis everything in life had felt important, urgent. Precious. And if he felt a connection with a woman well, then, perhaps he should just go for it. Take it as long and far as he could.

Except did he even know how long or far that could be. He didn't have a lot of options here. A lot of freedom.

He was, Chase reflected, a lousy deal.

Yet Millie only wanted this week, and really that should suit him perfectly. A week, he had.

A week, he would give.

And it would be the most incredible, intense week either of them had ever experienced.

'You OK there, Scary?'

She glanced at him, still looking dazed. 'Are you doing this on purpose?'

'What?'

'Pushing my buttons. Making me uncomfortable.'

He paused as if he had to think about it, which he didn't. 'Yes.'

She shook her head. 'OK, let me spell it out for you, Chase. I don't want to be pushed. I don't want buttons to be pressed. I want a week-long fling, some really great, mind-blowing sex, and that's *it*. And, if you don't think you can deliver, then maybe you should just take me back to shore right now.' She was trembling.

'Mind-blowing, huh?'

'Yes. Definitely.'

'I think I can deliver.'

'And nothing *more* than that,' she stressed, as if he didn't get it already.

'That's a problem.'

She blew out an impatient breath, pushing her hair behind her ears. She looked younger when she did that, although he guessed she was about his age, maybe a little younger. Mid-thirties, probably. 'Why is that a problem?'

'Because I don't think sex can be mind-blowing if a few buttons aren't pressed. In a manner of speaking, of course.'

She looked so disbelieving he almost winced. 'Are you telling me you haven't had cheap sex before? One-night stands? Flings?'

'No, I'm not saying that.' He'd had more than his share of all the above. He wasn't particularly proud of his past, standing on this side of it, but he'd own up to it.

'Then why are you insisting on something more now?'

He stretched his legs out in front of him, laced his hands behind his head. 'I suppose it depends on what you think of as more.'

'Stop talking in riddles.'

'OK, here it is, totally straight. We're both here for a week, right?'

'Right.'

'A week out of time, out of reality, and we'll never see each other again in New York or elsewhere. Yes?'

'Yes.'

'See, we *are* on the same page.'

'Spit it out,' she said, her teeth gritted, and he couldn't keep from grinning. He loved riling her.

'So you give me one week, and I give you mind-blowing sex. Deal?'

'I'm not signing until you tell me the fine print,' she said tautly, and he laughed aloud.

'You give me one week,' he repeated. He leaned forward, the urgency and excitement he felt coming out on his voice, his body. He felt it thrum between them with the pulse of an electric current. 'One week. Seven days. But you give me *everything*, Millie. You give me all of yourself, no holding back, no hiding. All in. And in return I give you mind-blowing.'

She stared at him silently for a long moment, her eyes wide, pupils dilated—with fear or desire? Probably both. Hell, he felt both. He couldn't believe he was doing this. He couldn't believe how much he wanted to.

'That,' she finally said, 'is a *lousy* deal.'

'You really think so?' He felt a tiny flicker of disappointment, but still that urgent hope. She was here. She was still talking, still wanting.

And, God knew, he wanted her. A lot.

'I told you I didn't want to get into messy emotional stuff. I don't want to *know* you, Chase.'

The flicker of disappointment deepened into actual hurt. He pushed it away. 'Except in the biblical sense, you mean.'

She let out a huff of exasperated breath. 'You're totally reneging on what we agreed on.'

'Nope. You are. My terms, remember?'

Her lips parted, realisation patently dawning. He waited. 'I thought you meant—well, the physical aspect of—of things. Like, maybe something a little bit kinky.' A beet-red blush washed over her face like a tide.

'We could go there if you like,' Chase offered. The prospect held an intriguing appeal. 'And I did say the when, where and how, it's true. But now I'm giving you some of those need-to-know details.'

She said nothing, just turned to stare out at the sea. They were in open water, the wind starting to die down. He should tack again, but he just waited. This moment was too important.

'I don't want to talk about my past,' she said slowly, forming each word with reluctance. 'I'll give myself in other ways, but not that.'

'That's kind of a big one.'

She turned to face him, and he felt as if a fist had struck his soul. She looked incredibly, unbearably bleak. 'Then you can take me back right now.'

Chase held her gaze, felt a twisting inside him. She was truly beautiful, he realised, but it was a stark, severe beauty, all clean angles and pure lines. And sadness. So much sadness. 'No need for that,' he said as lightly as he could. 'I agree.'

Her breath came out in a rush. 'Good.'

'So it's a deal?'

Her mouth trembled in an almost-smile. 'I guess it is.'

Chase stood up and walked towards the rigging. It was time to change direction. 'Then let our week begin.'

CHAPTER FIVE

MILLIE watched Chase steer the boat—he'd done something with the sail again—and tried to slow the hard beating of her heart. It was impossible.

She couldn't believe she had agreed. She couldn't believe she'd *wanted* to agree. They weren't her terms, not by a long shot, but maybe she could live with them. One week. No talking about the past. *Mind-blowing sex.*

Yes, she could live with them. Even if she felt a kind of numb terror at the thought of what lay ahead.

'So, are we going somewhere now?' she asked, rising from the bench to join him at the sail. This time she watched for the boom.

'Yep, land ahoy.' He pointed straight ahead to a crescent of sand amidst the water. It didn't look like much.

'What is that?'

'Our own version of *Survivor.*'

'You mean a deserted island?'

'I knew you were quick.'

'What are we going to do there?'

He gave her a knowing look. 'What do you think?' Millie gulped. Audibly. 'Relax, Millie. We're going to eat lunch.'

'Oh.' Another gulp. 'OK.'

'Although,' Chase mused as he navigated the boat towards that slice of beach, 'I almost think we should just do the nasty and get it over with, so you stop looking at me like I'm going to jump you at any second.'

She felt a flare of anticipation—and relief. 'Maybe that would be a good idea.'

Chase gave her another knowing look. 'I said almost.'

She folded her arms. 'Well, when are we going to—?'

'Need-to-know basis only,' Chase reminded her breezily. Then he was mooring the boat and the island—it really wasn't much—loomed before them.

He jumped out first, splashing through the shallows to moor the boat more securely, before turning to her and holding out his arms. 'Want to jump?'

She stood on the deck, one foot poised uncertainly on the railing, unsure just how she was going to get out of this thing. 'No, thank you.'

'I'll let it go this time, but remember our terms, Scary— you've got to give me everything.'

She stared at him, saw him looking both serious and smug, and then without warning or even thinking she took a flying leap from the boat and landed right on top of him. With a startled *'Oof!'* Chase fell back into the sea, pulling her with him. She was soaked instantly, and she felt the hard lines of his body press into her own soft curves. Excitement and awareness flared like rockets inside of her, obliterating thought.

Then through the sudden haze of her own desire she saw that Chase was wincing in what could only be pain. Mortification replaced lust and she tried to clamber off him. 'Did I hurt you—?'

'No.' He held her still on top of him and sucked in a breath. 'Surprised me, though.' He adjusted his arms around her, sliding his palms down her back so her hips rocked against his. 'Not that I mind.'

The water lapped around them, salty and warm. Her face

was inches from Chase's and she could see droplets of water clinging to his cheek and lips. Unable to resist touching him—and, really, why should she resist now?—she put the tip of her finger to one of the drops on Chase's cheek. He sucked in another breath, his gaze holding hers like a vise. Daringly, Millie touched another droplet on his lips. His mouth felt soft and warm, hard and cool all at the same time. Sensation zinged through her, frying her senses. Just one little touch and she was already drowning in a sea of desire.

Chase hadn't moved, just kept his hands on her hips, cradling her with aching closeness. She felt the hard thrust of his arousal against her thighs and instinctively shifted, though whether to bring him closer or farther away she didn't even know. Couldn't think.

The moment spun out and Millie felt the breath dry in her lungs as she waited for him to move.

And then he did.

'So.' Slowly, smiling, he eased her off him. 'Lunch.'

So they weren't going to go for it right then. She felt a bewildering mixture of disappointment and relief. Of course, he *had* said he preferred the moment before rather than after. There was still so much to look forward to.

Millie struggled up from of the water, watching as Chase rose out of the ocean like some archaic deity, water streaming in rivulets off the taut muscles of his back. He sluiced the water from his face and hair and then turned to her. 'You got a suit under there?'

'A suit?' She glanced down at the now-soaked striped top and capris her secretary had ordered her as part of her holiday wear. She hadn't had time to go shopping. 'Umm… No.'

'Shame. I was looking forward to seeing you in a string bikini.'

'I don't own a string bikini.'

'Let me guess—sensible one-piece.'

'I burn easily.'

'Remind me to apply another layer of sunscreen on you after lunch. But first, we dive.'

'Dive?' she repeated incredulously. 'But I just told you I don't have a swimsuit.'

Chase shrugged. 'You'll have to swim in your underwear. Or naked, if you prefer.'

'*What?*' This came out in a screech. Chase raised his eyebrows.

'Millie, we *are* going to sleep together, right? See each other naked? Touch each other in all those intimate places? Bring each other screaming to ecstasy?'

She was blushing. Like fire. *Way* too many details. 'That doesn't mean I want you to see me in my underwear in broad daylight,' she managed.

'Maybe I've decided to make love to you in broad daylight.' He pointed to the slender strip of sand. 'Maybe right there on that beach.'

Millie followed the direction of his pointing finger and could already see the two of them there on the beach, bodies naked, sandy and entwined. She could imagine it all too easily, no matter that she still felt shy about taking off her clothes. 'Even so,' she muttered. 'It's different.'

Chase let out a long-suffering sigh. 'So you want to swim in your clothes?'

'No.' She recrossed her arms, shifted her weight. She didn't know what she wanted. She'd agreed to this, she'd known it would be uncomfortable, and yet some bizarre and perverse part of herself still wanted it. Wanted him. Wanted the intimacy with him, even if she felt sick with nerves.

But if she really did want it why was she still resisting? Why was she fighting Chase on every little point? They'd already established he wasn't going to ask her about her past. They wouldn't see each other after this week.

They were going to have sex.

'Fine.' In one abrupt movement she slid her wet top over her head and kicked her way out of her capris. The clothes bobbed and floated on the surface of the sea, and belatedly she realised they were the only clothes she had here. She didn't relish the prospect of walking down the resort beach in her undies. Lifting her chin, she glared at him. 'Satisfied?'

'I wouldn't say I'm *satisfied*,' Chase said slowly, his gaze wandering over her in leisurely perusal. 'But pleased, yes.'

Millie shivered even though the air was sultry. She felt ridiculous standing there in her bra and panties, both a sensible, boring beige, even though Chase was only wearing a pair of shorts. They were both near-naked and yet...

When had someone last seen her this close to bare? A man? Rob, of course. Rob was the *only* man who had seen her in her underwear, besides her obstetrician. The thought was both absurd and excruciating.

Standing there under Chase's scrutiny, she was agonisingly conscious of all her faults. She was too skinny, due to the black-coffee breakfasts and skipped lunches. Her appetite had fallen off a cliff since the accident. And, while supermodels looked good stick-thin, Millie knew she didn't. Her hip bones were sharp and she'd dwindled down to an A-cup. And then of course there were the stretch marks, just two silver lines below her belly button—would he notice those? Would he ask?

No questions about her past. She'd remind him if necessary, and often.

Chase smiled and reached into the boat, bringing out two dive-masks. Millie eyed them dubiously.

'Why are we diving, anyway? I thought we were eating lunch.'

'We have to catch it first.'

Her jaw dropped. 'You have got to be kidding me.'

He arched an eyebrow. 'Do I look like a kidder?'

'Well, since you asked…'

'Seriously, it's easy. We're looking for conch—you know the big, pink shells? The pretty ones?' She nodded. 'We'll find a couple of those, I'll pry out the meat and we'll have conch salad. Delicious.'

'Raw?'

'Haven't you ever eaten sushi?'

'Only in a Michelin-starred restaurant in Soho.'

'Live a little, Millie.'

She frowned. 'I don't want to get food poisoning.'

'The lime juice in the dressing has enough acid to kill any nasties,' he assured her. 'I've eaten this loads of times.'

And just like that she could imagine him here, looking so easy and relaxed, with the kind of curvy blonde he usually dated. *She'd* have a string bikini. Or maybe she'd go bare. Either way Millie felt ridiculous standing there in her underwear, having no idea what to do. And, worse, she felt jealous.

Chase tossed her a mask. 'Look for the shells. We only need one or two.'

Dubiously she put the mask on. This was so out of her comfort zone, which was precisely why Chase had chosen to do it. When he'd said lunch she'd envisioned a picnic on the boat, gourmet finger-food and linen napkins. As if.

Still, she wouldn't give Chase the satisfaction of seeing just how uncomfortable she was. Squaring her shoulders, she adjusted her mask and followed Chase into the water. He was already cutting easily through the placid sea and with a deep breath Millie put her face in the water and gazed down into another world.

Rainbow-coloured fish darted in the shoals and amidst the rocks, prettier than any she'd seen in an aquarium. The sea water was incredibly clear, so the whole ocean floor seemed to open up in front of her, stretching on endlessly. Her lungs started to burn and she lifted her head to take a breath.

'You OK?' Chase had lifted his head too, and was glancing at her in concern.

'I'm fine.' She felt a strange stirring inside that he'd asked, something between gratitude and affection, that he was worried. He might be pushing her, but he wasn't going to let her fall.

And she wouldn't let herself either.

Chase kicked forward. 'Let's swim a little farther out.'

She followed him out into deeper water, and they swam and dove in silent synchronicity, the whole exercise surprisingly relaxing, until she finally saw a conch, pearly pink and luminescent, nestled against a rock. Taking a deep breath, she dove down and reached for it, her hand curving around its smooth shell as she kicked upwards to the surface.

Chase was waiting for her as she broke through. 'I got one!' Her voice rang out like an excited child's, and she gave him an all-too-sloppy grin.

'It's always a thrill. I got one too. That should be enough.'

They headed back to shore and Millie sat on the beach and watched while Chase retrieved a knife, cutting board and a few limes and shallots from the boat.

'You come prepared.'

'It's a quick, easy meal. But delicious.'

The sun dried her off, leaving salt on her skin as she sat with her elbows on her knees and watched him at work. She should have known he wouldn't let her sit back and do nothing for very long. Giving her a sideway glance, he beckoned her over.

'You can help.'

'You want me to slice some limes?' she asked hopefully, and he grinned.

'I thought you'd like a challenge. You can clean the conch.'

Bleh. Still, she wasn't going to argue. She eyed her wet tee-shirt drying on the boat, conscious that she was still only in her bra and pants. At least they were both sturdy and definitely not see-through. Chase caught her glance and shook his head.

'Your unmentionables are more modest than some of the bikinis I've seen, you know.'

'I'll bet.'

'Come on, Scary. You can do this.' He handed her a knife and instructed her on how to insert, twist and bring out the entire conch. Grimacing, Millie tried, and finally succeeded on her third try.

'Well done. Now we just need to fillet it. I'll do that, if you like.'

'Please.'

'You slice the limes.'

They worked in companionable silence for a moment, the sun warm on their backs. When everything had been sliced and diced, Chase fetched a wooden bowl from the boat and tossed it all together. He divided the salad between two plates and presented one to Millie with a courtly flourish.

'Your lunch, madam.'

'Thank you very much.' She took a bite, her eyes widening in surprise at how tasty it truly was. Chase smiled smugly.

'Told you.'

'Don't rub it in.' Unthinkingly she nudged him with her foot, a playful kick, and Chase raised his eyebrows. Too late Millie realised it could have looked like she was flirting. But she hadn't been, not intentionally anyway. She'd just been... enjoying herself.

And when was the last time she'd done that?

'A penny for your thoughts,' Chase said lightly. 'Or how about a bottle cap? I don't actually have any spare change.'

She glanced up and realised she'd been frowning. 'This is delicious, but it does seem a pity to eat such beautiful creatures.'

'They are pretty,' Chase agreed. 'They're actually endangered in US waters. But don't worry, they're still plentiful here. And the resort monitors the conch population around the island to make sure it never falls too low.'

'How eco-friendly of them. Is that a Bryant policy?'

He shrugged. 'A Chase Bryant policy. And economically friendly as well. If we don't conserve the island, there's no resort.'

Her salad finished, Millie propped her chin on her hands. 'But I thought you don't have anything to do with the resort.'

'Not really. But I'm interested in environmental policy, so…' He shrugged, but Millie wasn't fooled.

'Something happened?'

He tensed, and although it was barely noticeable Millie still felt it. Curiosity and a surprising compassion unfurled inside her. What had gone wrong between Chase and his family?

A second's pause was all it took for him to regain his usual lightness. 'Do I need to invoke the "no talking about the past" clause of our contract?'

'That was my past. Not yours.'

'I assumed it went both ways.'

She smiled sweetly. 'Fine print.'

Chase polished off the last mouthful of his meal before collecting their dishes and tossing them back into the boat. 'Fine. I was a bit of a reckless youth, made a few significant mistakes, and my father decided he'd rather I had nothing to do with the family business.' He shrugged, as if it were such ancient history that none of it mattered any more. 'So I went my own way, and am happy as a clam. Or a conch.'

Millie gazed at him, sensing the cracks in his armour.

He was just a little too deliberate with his light tone, and his story was far too simple. She wasn't about to press him, though. She'd been the one to insist that this week wasn't about emotional honesty or intimacy. But then, what *was* it about? It had been half a day already and they hadn't even kissed.

Yet she'd relaxed and enjoyed herself more than she'd ever thought possible.

'Come on,' Chase said, standing up and reaching a hand down to her. 'Let's explore the island.'

'That should take all of two minutes.'

'You'd be surprised.'

He hauled her to her feet, his strong, warm hand encasing hers, his fingers sliding over hers, skin on skin. Millie nearly shivered from the jolts that raced up and down her arm at that simple touch. When they did have sex, it was going to be amazing.

Mind-blowing.

Her heart slammed against her ribs as the realisation hit her again. Was she ready for this? Did she have any choice?

'Stop hyperventilating,' Chase said mildly. 'If it sets you at ease, I prefer a bed, or at least a comfortable surface. A beach seems romantic, but the sand can get into all sorts of inconvenient places.'

'You've tried it?' Millie tried not to feel nettled. *Jealous.* She'd never had sex on a beach.

'Once or twice,' Chase answered with a shrug. He was leading her away from the boat, towards a small grove of palm trees. 'Trust me, it's overrated.'

Millie's mind buzzed. OK, a bed. What bed? Her bed at the resort? At his villa? How were they going to *do* this? Well, obviously she knew *how*, but how without it being completely awkward or embarrassing? She hadn't had sex in over two years and then only ever with one man. What on earth had she been thinking, suggesting a fling? She was the least flingy person she knew.

She also knew it was way too late to be thinking this way. She should have considered all the uncomfortable practicalities before she'd made the suggestion to Chase. Before they'd agreed on a deal.

Before she'd suddenly realised just what this all meant, and that there was no such thing as simple sex.

Yet, even though she *was* hyperventilating, she knew she didn't want to back out. She wanted Chase.

Did his sailboat have a bed?

'Yes,' Chase called back and Millie skidded to a halt right there in the trees.

'What do you mean, *yes*?'

He stopped and turned, so aggravatingly amused. 'Yes, the sailboat has a bed.'

Her jaw dropped. 'Did I say that out loud?'

'No, but I could follow your thought process from here. I hate to say it, but you're kind of predictable.'

'You didn't expect me to jump on top of you from the boat,' Millie pointed out, and Chase cocked his head.

'True. I like when you surprise me.'

She'd liked it too. She'd liked feeling his hard body under hers. She'd enjoyed touching him. Just thinking about it now made her blood heat and her body pulse. Why was she waiting for him to kiss her? What if she kissed him?

'Don't get ahead of yourself there,' Chase murmured. 'Our first kiss needs to be special.'

She let out a most inelegant snort. 'What are you, a mind reader?'

'You were staring at my lips like they were the latest stock market report. It didn't take a huge amount of mental ability to guess what you were thinking.'

Disgruntled, she tugged her hand from his. 'So where are we going, exactly?'

Chase took her hand back, folding her fingers in his once more. 'I'll show you.'

They walked through the palms for a few more minutes, wending their way through the drooping fronds, the ground sandy beneath their feet. Then Chase stopped, slipping his arm around Millie's waist to draw her to his side. He did it so easily, so assuredly, that she didn't even think about any awkwardness as her leg lay warm against his, his fingers splayed along her hip.

'Look.'

She looked and saw a perfect little pool right there in the middle of the trees, a tiny jewel-like oasis, its surface as calm as a mirror. Millie knelt down and cupped the water with two hands; it was clear and cool. She glanced up at Chase. 'It's fresh?'

'Yep, fed by an underground spring, I think.' She shook her head in wonder, amazed that such a tiny island would have a source of fresh water. 'Drink,' Chase said. 'I've drunk it before, it tastes great. You could sell it for five bucks a bottle in the city.'

She took a sip, suddenly self-conscious at how Chase was watching her. When had taking a drink of water become sensual? Provocative?

'You know what the most amazing thing is, though?' he said, and she sat back on her heels.

'What?'

'You've been walking around in your underwear for most of the day and you haven't even noticed.'

She let out an embarrassed little laugh. 'And, now that you've reminded me, I'm going to notice.'

He grinned. 'Actually, what I was really going to say is that a couple of hundred years ago there were some shipwrecked sailors on a little atoll just a few hundred yards away, without any fresh water. They didn't discover this place and they died of thirst.'

She dropped her hands. 'That's awful.'

'I know. If they'd just tried swimming around a little bit, or even making a raft or something, they might have survived.' He shook his head. 'But they were just too scared.'

Millie narrowed her eyes. 'And I'm supposed to make the connection, right?'

He stared at her in exaggerated innocence. 'Connection?'

She stood up. 'If those sailors had just been a little more adventurous, they would have survived. Really lived. All they had to do was swim a little farther than they were comfortable with.'

'I don't think they could swim at all, actually. Most sailors back then couldn't.'

She folded her arms. 'I don't need the morality tale.'

'It was obvious, huh?'

'Like a sledgehammer.'

'And I made the whole thing up to boot.'

She let out a huff of outraged laughter. 'You did?'

'No, I didn't. It's actually true. Well, a legend around here anyway.' He grinned and Millie didn't know whether to throttle him or kiss him. She felt like doing both, at the same time.

'You're unbelievable.'

'So I've been told.'

His gaze rested on her like a heavy, palpable thing, assessing, understanding. Knowing. She drew a breath.

'Look, Chase, I know I'm uptight and you think I need to relax. I probably seem like a joke to you.'

'You don't,' Chase said quietly. 'I promise you, Millie, this is no joke.'

She looked away, discomfited by the sudden intensity in

his voice. 'I don't want to be your project,' she said quietly. 'The reckless playboy teaches the uptight workaholic how to relax and have fun. Shows her how to really live.' She bit her lip hard, surprised by the sudden catch of tears in her throat. 'That isn't what I want from you.'

Chase took a step closer to her. 'Then maybe you should tell me what you do want.'

She forced herself to meet his gaze. 'Mind-blowing sex, remember?'

'I remember. And I remember the deal we made. One week, and you give me everything.'

He'd come closer, close enough so she could feel the heat of him, inhaled the scent that she was starting to realise was just Chase. Sun and musk and male. She drew a shaky breath. 'I don't know how much I have to give.'

He touched her chin with her hand, his fingers like a whisper against her skin. 'Someone hurt you. I get that. But this can be different, Millie.'

She shook her head, swallowed the hot lump of tears. 'No one hurt me, Chase. Not the way you think.'

'No questions about the past, I know,' he said, the hint of a smile in his voice. 'And this week isn't meant to be some lesson. It's just us—enjoying each other.'

Her breath came out in a soft hiss. 'OK.'

He stroked her cheek, and she had to fight not to close her eyes and surrender to that little caress. 'And I enjoy seeing you open up like a flower in the sun. I like seeing your face surprised by a smile.'

'Don't.'

'Is that scary, Millie? Is that out of your comfort zone?'

She swallowed. 'Yes.'

His other hand came up to cradle her face, just as he had last night. Had it only been last night? She felt as if she'd known this man for years. And he knew her.

'How long has it been,' he asked, 'since you were happy?'

'Two years.' The answer slipped out before she could think better of it. 'But really longer. Two years since I've known.' She stared at him, knowing he was drawing more from her than she'd ever intended to give, and also knowing that she wanted to give it. One week. For one week she wanted intimacy. Physical, emotional, intense. All of it. *All in*.

Chase was gazing back at her, his expression both tender and fierce, and then slowly, deliberately, he dipped his head and brushed his lips with her own.

A soft sigh of surrender escaped her as her lips parted underneath his. His lips were all the things she'd thought they would be: soft, hard, cool, warm. And so achingly gentle.

He brushed his lips across hers a second and third time, like a greeting. Then he touched his tongue to the corner of her mouth, and then the other corner, as if he were asking her how she was. A wordless conversation of mouths. Her lips parted wider, accepting. *I'm good.*

He deepened the kiss, his hands tightening as they cradled her face, and Millie's hands came up to bunch on the bare skin of his shoulders. Yet even as sensation swirled through her another part of her was stepping back and analysing everything.

His hands felt bigger than Rob's. His body was harder. His kiss was more demanding and yet more gentle at the same time. More assured. Yet could she even remember the last time she and Rob had kissed? That last day, all she'd had were harsh words, impatient sighs...

She hadn't even said goodbye.

Chase lifted his head, pulling back a little bit so Millie blinked in surprise. 'Your lack of response is a bit of a buzz-kill, you know.'

'What?' She gaped like a fish. 'I wasn't—'

'No,' Chase agreed, 'you weren't. It started off rather nicely, but then you went somewhere else in your head.' She couldn't deny it, and his gaze narrowed. 'What were you thinking about, Millie?' She swallowed, said nothing. 'You were thinking about some other guy, weren't you?'

'No!' Millie protested, then bit her lip. She couldn't lie, not to Chase. 'I couldn't help it.'

For the first time since she'd seen him, he looked angry. Or maybe even hurt. Emotion flashed in his eyes like thunder and then he deliberately relaxed. 'I know you think too much. You've got to turn off that big brain of yours, Millie.'

'I know.' Did she ever. The whole reason she'd embarked on this fling of theirs was to keep herself from thinking. Remembering. Tormenting herself with guilty regrets.

'Let's go back to the boat,' Chase said. 'We should get back to St Julian's before dark.'

Silently Millie followed him back through the grove to the slender beach and then onto the boat. Chase didn't so much as look back at her once, or help her onto the boat. Any warmth between them seemed to have evaporated. Millie fetched her clothes, now thankfully dry but stiff as a board and caked with salt, and clutched them to her. She stood uncertainly on the deck while Chase set the boat free from its moorings, his movements taut with suppressed energy—or emotion? Was he angry with her?

'Is there somewhere I can change?'

'Don't bother.' He didn't even look at her as he reached for another line.

'What?' She didn't like seeing Chase this way, the hard lines of his face transformed into harshness—or maybe just indifference. Gone was the charming, charismatic man she'd come to like—and trust. 'I don't want to walk into the resort in my underwear,' she said, trying to joke, but Chase turned to her with a dangerously bland expression.

'You can put your clothes on after.'

'After?'

'After we have sex. That's what you wanted, isn't it, Millie? No messy emotions or entanglements, no getting to know each other.' He spread his arms wide, a cool smile curling his mouth. 'Well, here we are. Alone in an ocean, and there's a perfectly good bed in the cabin below. No reason not to hop to it.'

Millie stared, swallowed. 'You mean now?'

'Right now.' He jerked a thumb in direction of the ladder that led below deck. 'Let's go.'

CHAPTER SIX

WHAT the hell was he doing? Being a total bastard, judging by the look of shocked horror on Millie's face. But he was angry, even if he shouldn't be. The thought of Millie thinking of some other jerk while he was pouring his soul into that kiss filled him with a blind rage.

'Well?' Chase arched an eyebrow and put his hands on his hips. 'What are you waiting for?'

Her teeth sank into those worry marks on her lower lip. She clutched her clothes tighter to her chest. 'Somehow, with the way you're looking at me, I don't think it's going to be mind-blowing.'

'Leave that to me.'

She shook her head. 'I don't like angry sex.'

He gave her a level look. 'I'm not angry.' He wasn't, he realised with a flash of cringing insight. He was hurt. He hadn't expected to care so much, so quickly.

Millie gave just as level a look back, even as her eyes flashed fire. He might not be angry, but she was. Well, fine. Bring it on.

'All right.' She lifted her chin a notch, her eyes still flashing, and stalked past him to the ladder. Chase watched her descend below deck, her body taut and quivering with tension. Or maybe anger, or even fear.

Did it matter? Wasn't this what she wanted, a quick bout

of meaningless sex? She could get him out of her system, or so she undoubtedly hoped.

And maybe he'd get her out of his. He'd spent the afternoon coaxing smiles from her even as he enjoyed himself more than he'd ever thought possible. Every smile, every laugh, had felt like a discovery. A victory.

He thought they were building something—admittedly something fragile and temporary, but *still*. Something. And the whole time she'd been thinking of some stupid ex.

'Are you coming?' she called from below, her voice as taut as her body had been.

Chase's mouth curved grimly at the unwitting *double entendre*. 'You'd better believe it.'

He hauled himself down the ladder and saw that Millie stood in front of the double bed. She turned to him, her chest heaving, her nipples visible beneath the thin, silky material of her bra. She arched her eyebrows and curved her mouth in a horrible rictus smile.

'All right, Chase. Let's see what you've got.'

He swallowed, acid churning in his gut. How had they got here? The afternoon had been full of tenderness and teasing, and now they were acting like they hated each other.

Millie's eyes glittered and he knew she wouldn't back down. She never backed down from a challenge; he'd learned that already.

And hell if he'd back down either. She was the one who had said she didn't want to get to know him. Wasn't interested in emotional anything. Right now, right here, he could give her what she wanted. The only thing she wanted.

And, damn it, he'd want it too.

'Take off your bra.' A pulse beat hard in the hollow of her throat but she undid it and tossed it to the floor. Her breasts were small and round, high and firm. Perfect. Chase swallowed. 'And the rest.' She glared at him as she kicked off her underwear, her chin still tilted high.

'Is this what you call foreplay?'

He almost laughed. She was magnificent. Naked, proud, defiant, *strong*. He shook his head. 'I just like to see what I get in this deal of ours.'

'Only fair I get the same opportunity, then.'

He arched an eyebrow, aroused in spite of the anger. Or maybe because of it. Hell, he didn't know anything any more. 'What are you saying, Scary?'

'Take off your pants.'

He did.

They stared at each other almost in grim silence, both of them totally naked, nothing between them. The air seemed to crackle with the tension, with the expectation.

Hell.

What now?

Millie folded her arms. Waited. Chase felt like a circus seal, or a damn monkey. She clearly expected him to *perform*.

He hadn't wanted it to be this way. He'd wanted to gain her trust, even her affection, and help her to lose control in the most amazing way possible. Right now she was clinging to that precious control with her french-manicured fingernails and it was slipping crazily away from him.

He didn't want this.

He wasn't going to back down.

'Get on the bed.'

She gave him a little smirk, almost as if he were being *so* predictable, and lay on the bed. She even put her hands behind her head as if she were incredibly relaxed, but she was trembling.

Damn.

Again Chase hesitated. *Don't do this.* He didn't want to

ruin what they had by losing her trust, affection, *everything*, in a bout of absurdly unsexy sex. Except who was he kidding? They didn't *have* anything.

This was all they had—this, right here on the bed.

'Let me tell you,' Millie drawled, her hands still laced behind her head, 'this is turning out to be the worst sexual encounter of my life, and forget about mind-blowing.'

Chase saw that she still trembled.

He sat on the edge of the bed and slowly ran his hand from the arch of her foot along her calf to behind her knee, his fingers instinctively seeking further, finding the soft, smooth skin of her inner thigh. More softness. He felt her muscles tense and quiver beneath his touch. Her breath hitched.

'I'm not going to play this game,' he said quietly and she stared at him, her whole body going rigid.

'This was *your* idea.'

'Yeah, I'll grant you that. But you went for it because this is what you want.'

'You think *this* is what I want?'

'There's no emotional intimacy or getting to know you in this scenario, is there?' He slid his hand higher, savouring the sweet softness of her thigh. Another couple of inches would be even sweeter.

She stared at him, mesmerised, trapped. He stilled his hand. 'You know I'm right, Millie.'

In answer she reached up, lacing her fingers behind his head, and pulled him down for a hungry, open-mouthed kiss. Her tongue delved inside and she arched upwards, pressing her body against him.

Shock short-circuited Chase's brain for a second. Then his libido ramped up and he kissed her back just as hungrily with an instinct he was helpless to repress—even as he acknowledged this wasn't what he wanted. He didn't even think it was what Millie wanted, not deep down. She was trying to stay in control, seizing it desperately, and he couldn't let her.

But then her hand wrapped around him and he stopped thinking about what he couldn't do. His body was telling him what he could.

'Millie.' Her name was a groan against her mouth and he reached up to try to remove her death grip on the back of his head. *'Wait...'*

But she didn't want to wait. She was all over him, eager, urgent, desperate, making him feel the same way. His self-control was slipping away. How did a man argue for a more emotional experience when the woman beneath him was determined to drive him wild? For the feel of Millie's hands on him, her legs hooked around his hips as she angled upwards, was making him crazy. Through the fog of his own lust he tried to remember where he'd put the condoms.

'Quickly...' Millie whispered, her voice a ragged whimper, and Chase stilled. He heard too much desperation and even sadness in her voice, and he didn't want that. No matter how much his body screamed otherwise.

'Millie.' He pushed away from her a little bit, enough to see her pale, dazed face. 'Let's hold on a moment, shall we?' he said unevenly, even though his greatest desire at that point was to forget emotion and sensitivity, and even a condom, and just drive right into her.

'No, I don't want...' Her face went a shade paler, and then she lurched upwards. 'I think I'm going to be sick.' In one abrupt movement she rolled off the bed and raced to the head. Chase listened to her retching into the toilet in a kind of stunned disbelief.

This was starting to feel like the worst sexual encounter of his life too. He reached for his shorts and pulled them on, grabbed a spare tee-shirt from the drawer and waited on the edge of the bed.

A few minutes later a pale and shaky-looking Millie emerged. From somewhere Chase found a smile. 'I don't think that was because of the conch.'

She gave him a rather wobbly smile back, although her eyes were dark with pain. 'No, it wasn't.' Somehow the anger, tension and even the desperation of moments before had evaporated, but Chase didn't know what was left. He felt bewildered, like someone had skipped ahead in the scene selection on a DVD. He was clearly missing some plot points to this story.

'Here.' He handed her the tee-shirt and she slipped it on. Her hair was tousled, the shirt falling to mid-thigh. With a little sigh she sat on the edge of the bed, about as far away from him as possible.

'Sorry about that.'

'To which part of the evening are you referring?' he quipped, parroting her own words from last night back to her.

Millie gave a tiny, tired smile and leaned her head against the wall. She closed her eyes and with a pang of remorse Chase saw how exhausted she looked. Today had been quite the rollercoaster.

'To the part where I threw up in your bathroom a few minutes ago.'

'On a boat it's called a head.'

'Whatever.' She opened her eyes. 'That was another buzz-kill, I suspect.'

'To say the least.' They stared at each other, unspeaking, but Chase was surprised at how *un*-awkward it seemed. Maybe you got to a point with a person where things didn't seem so embarrassing or strange. If so, he'd got to that point pretty quickly with Millie. 'You want to tell me what's going on?'

'Remember the no-talking clause?'

'That clause was voided when you threw up. I was about six seconds from being inside you, Millie.'

She bit her lip and he reached over and gently touched those worry marks. 'You're going to get a scar from doing that if you don't cut it out.'

She sighed and shook her head. 'Maybe this whole thing was a bad idea, Chase.'

He felt a lurch of what could only be alarm. He didn't like feeling it. At this point, he should be agreeing with her. This *was* a bad idea. Neither of them needed the kind of mind games this week seemed to play on them. He'd convinced himself he wanted intense, but this? This was way too much.

Yet even so he heard himself saying, 'Why do you say that?'

'Because I'm not ready.'

She'd felt pretty ready beneath him. With effort Chase yanked his thoughts from that unhelpful direction. 'Ready?' he repeated.

'For this. A fling, an affair, whatever you want to call it. I wanted to be ready, I wanted to move on, but I don't know if I can. I can't stop thinking—' She stopped abruptly, shook her head.

It was no more than he'd already guessed, yet he didn't like hearing it. Didn't like thinking that some guy still owned her heart and mind so much he couldn't even get a toe-in. Jealousy. That was what he felt, pure and simple. Determinedly Chase pushed it away. 'We went about this all wrong, Scary,' he said. 'And that was my fault. I'm sorry.'

Surprise flashed across her features, like the first beam of sunlight after a downpour. 'For what?'

'For getting angry. I didn't like the fact that you were thinking of whatever guy did a number on you when I was kissing you.' He smiled wryly. 'It's kind of an insult to, you know, my masculinity.'

'Sorry.'

'It's OK. I should have got over it. Instead I pushed you—and myself—in a direction I had no intention of going.'

Her mouth curved in the faintest of smiles. 'Angry sex, huh?'

'It's really not that great.'

'Kind of like sex on a beach.'

'Exactly. Both overrated.' He sighed and raked his hand through his hair. 'Look, let's hit rewind on this evening. Go back on deck and forget this happened.'

'Well,' she said, sounding almost mischievous, 'I don't think I'm going to forget the sight of you naked in a hurry.'

Chase grinned. 'Me neither, Scary. Me neither.' Still smiling, he reached for her hand and felt a clean sweep of thankfulness when she took it. How bizarre that all that tension, anger and hurt had melted and reformed into something else. Something deeper and truer. Friendship.

'I hope,' Millie said as he led her from the cabin, 'we're not diving for dinner.'

'Definitely not.' He felt himself warm from the inside out, and he gave her hand a squeeze before helping her up the ladder.

Millie walked to the cushioned bench in the back of the boat on wobbly legs. She felt exhausted, both emotionally and physically, by the events of the day and especially the last hour. Chase Bryant was putting her through the wringer. Or maybe she was doing it to herself, by trying to have the desperate, mindless sex she'd thought she wanted until her body had rebelled and thrown up a whole lot of conch.

Chase was right, of course. It wasn't the conch that had made her sick. It was the memories. She couldn't turn her brain off, as much as she wanted to. Couldn't stop remembering, regretting. She'd wanted to have this fling so she could forget, but it wasn't happening that way at all. It was making things worse. Chase was opening up things inside her, stirring to life everything she'd wanted to be forgotten and buried, *gone*.

She watched as he set sail, part of her mind admiring the lean strength of his tanned, muscled body even as the rest whirled and spun in confusion. She hadn't expected him to become so angry earlier. And she hadn't expected him to be so understanding just then.

For a moment there on the bed, the cabin silent except for the draw and sigh of their own breathing, she'd actually wanted to tell him things. Confide all her confusion, sadness and guilt. But that would mean telling him about Rob. About Charlotte. And she never spoke about Charlotte. Even now the pain ripped through her, all too fresh even though it had been two years. Two years since the phone call that had torn her world apart, taken everyone she loved.

Shouldn't two years be enough time for the scars to heal? To finally feel ready to move on?

She felt the cushion dip beneath her and blinked to see Chase sitting next to her. She'd been so lost in her own miserable thoughts she hadn't seen him coming.

He touched her mouth and even now, after everything that had and hadn't happened, she felt that quiver of awareness, the remnant of desire. 'Scars, Scary. I'm serious.'

She let out a trembling little laugh. 'It's hard to stop something you're not even aware you're doing.'

'What deep thoughts are making you bite your lip?'

'They're not particularly deep.' She turned a little bit away from him, forcing him to drop his hand. 'Are we heading back to the resort?'

'No. To my villa.'

She turned back to him, felt a frisson of—what? Not fear. Not excitement. No, this felt strange and suddenly she knew why. She felt hope. Even after the absolute disaster below deck, Chase was giving her—*them*—a second chance.

'What are we going to do there?'

He regarded her speculatively for a moment. 'I'm going to cook for you while you soak in my jacuzzi. Then we're going to eat the fantastic meal I've whipped up, watch a movie, maybe have a glass of wine. Or sparkling water, as the case may be.'

'That sounds surprisingly relaxing.'

'Glad you think so.'

'And then?'

'And then we'll go to sleep in my very comfortable, king-sized bed and I'll hold you all night long.'

He spoke breezily enough, yet Millie heard the heartfelt sincerity underneath the lightness, and she felt tears sting her eyes. She blinked hard.

'Why are you being so nice to me?'

'Hasn't a man been nice to you before, Millie?' He spoke quietly, as if he felt sad for her. She shook her head.

'Don't pity me, Chase. I've—I've had a perfectly fine relationship before.'

'That sounds incredibly boring and unromantic, but OK. Good for you.'

She let out a trembling laugh. He *never* let up, but then neither did she. 'This doesn't sound very intense, though,' she told him. 'I thought this week was all about excitement.'

'There are different kinds of intense. And I think a quiet evening at home will be intense enough for you.'

He rose from the bench and Millie watched as he steered the boat, one hand on the tiller. The wind ruffled his short hair, his eyes narrowed against the setting sun. He paused, his hand still on the tiller, to watch the glorious descent of that orb of fire towards the now-placid sea. Shock jolted through her because for a moment Chase looked like she felt. Desperate. Sad. Longing to hope.

Then he straightened his shoulders and turned back to her with a smile, all lightness restored. 'Almost there.'

Half an hour later Millie was soaking in the most opulent tub she'd ever seen, huge, sunken and made of black marble. Chase had filled it right to the top with steaming water, half a bottle of bubble bath, and then left not one but two thick, fluffy towels on the side. Then with a smile and a salute he'd closed the door and gone to cook dinner.

When, Millie wondered, had she ever felt so incredibly pampered? So *loved*?

She froze, even in all that hot, fragrant water. *Don't even think that,* she told herself. *Don't go there.* The dreaded L-word. She'd loved Rob. She'd loved Charlotte. And here she was, two years later, heartbroken and alone.

She slipped beneath the foaming water and scrubbed the sand from her hair. The thoughts from her mind. She wanted to enjoy this evening, all the lovely things Chase had promised her. It had been so long since she'd had anything like this.

Since she'd felt anything like this.

Don't think. One week. That was all they had, all she wanted to have. One week of enjoyment, of fun and, yes, of sex. Despite today's disaster they could still have it. Enjoy it.

And then walk away. Move on, just like she wanted to, because anything else—anything real or lasting—was way too frightening. She'd loved once. Lost once. And it wasn't going to happen again.

One week suited her perfectly. One intense, wonderful week.

When Millie came out of the bathroom she saw, to her surprise, her suitcase laid out by the bed. How on earth had Chase been able to get into her room and take her stuff?

The answer was obvious: he was a Bryant. For a little while there she'd forgotten; he'd just been Chase. Annoyance and affection warred within her. It was nice to have her clothes, but it was a little *too* thoughtful. Sighing, she discarded her towel and reached for one of the boring outfits her secretary had chosen, this one a beige linen dress with short sleeves and no shape. She glanced down at it and gave a grimace of disgust. She wished, suddenly and fiercely, that she owned something sexy.

But then she'd never owned anything sexy. She and Rob hadn't been about sexy. Their sex life had been good enough, certainly, but they had both been so focused. There had been no time or inclination for sexy or silly or fun.

Everything that Chase was.

Was that why she'd chosen him for her first fling? Because, despite initial appearances, he was utterly unlike her husband?

Her thoughts felt too tangled to separate or understand. And maybe, like Chase said, she was over-thinking this. Straightening the boring dress, Millie headed out into the rest of the villa.

It was a gorgeous house, made of a natural stone that blended into its beach-side surroundings, the inside all soaring space and light. She found Chase in the gourmet kitchen that flowed seamlessly into the villa's main living space with scattered leather sofas and a huge picture-window framing an expanse of sand and sky.

'That smells delicious.'

'Chicken with pineapple and mango salsa,' Chase informed her, whipping a dish cloth from his shoulder to wipe something up on the granite work surface. Millie felt her heart—or something—squeeze at the sight of him. He'd changed into a worn blue tee-shirt and faded jeans, and he

looked so natural and relaxed standing there, different bowls
and pans around him, the smells of fruit and spice in the air.

She and Rob had never cooked. They'd eaten takeaway
every night or ready-made meals from the gourmet super-
market. Why cook, Rob had used to say, if you don't have
to? And she had agreed. After a ten-hour day at work, the
last thing she felt like doing was making a meal. And they'd
both been proud of the way Charlotte, at only two years old,
would eat all the things they ate. Brie and smoked salmon.
Spicy curries and pad thai. She'd loved it all.

A knot of emotion lodged in Millie's throat. Why was
she thinking about Charlotte? She never did. She'd closed
that part of herself off, shut up in a box marked *'do not
open'*. Ever.

Yet here she was, memories springing unbidden into her
mind, filling up her heart.

'Millie?' Chase was glancing at her, eyes narrowed. 'You
OK there, Scary?'

She nodded. Sniffed. How stupidly revealing of her, but
she couldn't help it. She'd thought she could handle this
week, but already she was finding she couldn't. She was
thinking too much. Feeling too much. She'd thought Chase
would make her forget, but instead he was helping her to
remember.

'That bath was wonderful,' she said, in a deliberate and
obvious effort to change the subject. 'I could live in it for
a week.'

'The water might get a bit cold.' Chase reached for a
couple of green chilies and began dicing them with practised ease.

'Fair point.' She took a breath and decided she needed
to get on firmer footing. Find a little distance. 'As nice as
it is to wear my own clothes, I'm not sure how they got in
your bedroom.'

'A very nice bell hop drove them over while you were in the tub.'

'Don't you think you could have asked?'

He glanced up, eyebrows arched. 'Are we still going over this? My terms, remember?'

'You can't keep throwing that at me every time I object to something, Chase.'

'And that is because…?'

She blew out an exasperated breath. 'It's not fair.'

'True.'

'*So?*'

'We're not playing baseball, Millie. Or Parcheesi. There are no rules.'

She folded her arms. 'Are you on some huge power trip? Is that what this is about?'

'Does it seem like it?' He sounded genuinely curious, and Millie was compelled to an unwilling honesty.

'No, which is why I don't get it. I still don't really get what you want, Chase. Most men would take the sex and run.'

'Has that been your experience?'

'*Don't* go there. No questions about the past.'

'I told you what I wanted. One week.'

'One intense, all-in week.'

'Only kind that works for me.'

'*Why?*'

Chase didn't answer for a moment. He concentrated on his cooking, taking out some pieces of chicken from the bowl of marinade and tossing them into a pan shimmering with hot oil. Millie listened to the sizzle and spat as they cooked, a delicious aroma wafting up from the pan.

'Why not?' he finally said and flipped the chicken. 'I know it's easier and simpler on the surface, Millie, just to skim life. Don't dig too deeply. Don't feel too much. I've been there. That's most of my misspent youth.'

She swallowed, knowing he was right. Easier, simpler and safer. 'But now?'

'I want something more. I want the whole *carpe diem* thing. Seize life. Suck the marrow from its bones.'

'For one week.'

'Yep. That's about the size of it.'

'And you decide to do this with me?' She couldn't keep the disbelief from her voice. 'When you must know I'm the exact opposite of all that?'

He gave her a decidedly roguish smile. 'That makes it more fun. And all the more reason why it has to be on my terms. Otherwise we'd never get anywhere.'

Millie shook her head. How could she argue with him? How could she explain that she was afraid one week with Chase might be enough to peel back all her protective layers, leave her bare, exposed and hurting? She didn't want to admit the possibility even to herself.

She slid onto a stool and braced her elbows on the counter. 'So what made you change your mind? To stop skimming?'

He poured the rest of the marinade on top of the chicken, stirring it slowly. 'I think I might take this opportunity to invoke part B of the no-talking-about-the-past clause, which details that I don't have to talk about it either.'

'You have something to hide?'

She almost missed the dark flash in his eyes. She knew he was touchy about his family, but he'd told her the basics about that. Was there something else? Something he didn't want her to know?

'Not really,' he said, taking the lid off a pan of rice and spooning some onto two plates warming on the hob. 'Just some things I'd rather not talk about.'

'What about your youth was so misspent?'

'You trying to get to *know* me?'

'Maybe.'

He shrugged. 'Just the usual, really, for a spoiled rich kid. Expelled from half a dozen boarding schools, crashed my father's Maserati. The final straw was sleeping with his girlfriend.' He spoke so very nonchalantly, yet Millie sensed a thread of self-protectiveness in his voice. Maybe even hurt.

'That's pretty misspent.'

'Yeah, well, I like to do things right.' Now he ladled the chicken in its fragrant sauce over the rice, and Millie had to admit it all looked delicious. The man could cook.

'And what made you change? I assume you're not crashing Maseratis now?'

'Only the odd one here or there.'

'Seriously.'

'You want me to be serious?' He let out a long-suffering sigh and handed her a plate. 'In that case, I need sustenance.'

They sat in a dining alcove, the floor-to-ceiling windows giving an endless view of the ocean darkening to damson under a twilit sky.

'Your favourite part of the day,' Chase said softly, and a thrill ran through her—a thrill at the thought that this man was starting to *know* her. And that she liked it.

How terrifying.

'So?' Millie said, attempting to banish that thrill. 'Why the change?'

Chase speared a piece of chicken. 'Remember I told you my father decided he didn't want me in the family business?'

'That was, I assume, after the girlfriend incident?'

'Correct. That, of course, just made me more determined to be as bad as I could be.'

'How old were you?'

'Seventeen.'

Millie felt a surprising tug of sympathy for the teenaged Chase. Normally she'd just roll her eyes at even the thought of some spoiled rich kid going through cars and women at a break-neck speed, but when she knew it was Chase… When she knew he wasn't shallow or spoiled, had more depth than most people she met… Well, it felt different. She felt different.

'So you were super-bad, then?'

'More of the same, really. Parties, cars, women, drink. Some recreational drug use I'm definitely not proud of.' He still spoke lightly, but she saw shadows in his eyes. Felt them in her heart. What a sad, empty life. And her life, in a totally different way, had been sad and empty too. *Still was.*

'So what was your life-changing moment?'

He gave her a speculative glance. 'This is getting pretty personal.'

She swallowed and decided not to dissemble. 'I know.'

Chase speared another bit of chicken and chewed slowly before answering. 'My father died. I was finishing college, I'd been studying architecture more for the hell of it than anything else. I was still pretty much a waste of space.' He paused, and Millie almost reached out to him, touched him, even just a hand on his arm. She stopped herself and Chase continued.

'I found out from his will that he'd legally disowned me from inheriting anything. Cut me out completely. It was what he'd threatened to do years before, but I guess I didn't really believe he meant it until then. And, while I have to admit I was pretty disappointed that I wouldn't be getting any of his money, I felt something worse.' He glanced away, his expression shuttering. 'Disappointment. Disappointment in myself, and how little I'd made of my life.'

Then Millie couldn't stop herself. *All in, right?* She reached across the table and touched Chase's hand, just a whisper of her fingers against his, but it was big for her and she thought he knew that. He glanced down at their touching hands and then looked up, smiling wryly.

'Not that inspiring a story, really.'

'Actually, it is. You recognised your mistakes and did something about them. Most people don't get that far.'

'Did you?'

The blunt question startled her. All this intimacy and sharing was great until he turned the tables on her. She withdrew her hand. 'Maybe, in a manner of speaking.' She paused, her fingers clenching into an involuntary fist. 'But it was too late.'

'Why was it too late, Millie?' She shook her head. She'd said too much. 'All these secrets,' Chase said lightly. 'You know it only makes you more intriguing, right? Sexier too. And it makes me want to find out what you're hiding.'

'Trust me, it's not sexy. Or intriguing. It's just…' She let out a breath. 'Sad. In a lot of different ways. And the reason I don't want to tell you is because you'll look at me differently.'

'Would that be a bad thing?'

'Yes, it would.' She liked the way Chase teased her. Riled her. Yes, he made her uncomfortable, but he also made her feel real and alive. He didn't tiptoe around her feelings, didn't tinge every smile with pity or uncertainty. Didn't look at her like she was a walking tragedy.

The way everyone else did.

Maybe *that* was what had attracted her to him in the first place—the fact that he didn't really know her at all. And yet, Millie had to acknowledge, he did know her. The real her. He just didn't know what had happened in her life.

And she liked it that way.

Yet how could he really know her, without knowing that?

Tired of the tangle of her thoughts, she rose from the table. 'Didn't you say something about a movie?'

Fifteen minutes later, after friendly bickering about whether to see an action flick or worthy drama, they settled on a DVD. Chase sat down on the sofa and before Millie could debate where to sit he pulled her down next to him, fit her snugly next to him and draped his arm around her shoulders. Millie tensed for just a second and then relaxed into Chase's easy embrace. Why was she fighting this? The weight of his arm and the solid strength of his body felt good.

She tried to pay attention to the movie—the worthy drama she had insisted upon—but she was so tired that her eyelids were drooping halfway through. She must have dozed off, for some time later she stirred to find herself being scooped up in Chase's arms.

'I can't believe I sat through something with subtitles so you could fall asleep on me,' Chase said, and there was so much affection in his voice that Millie curled naturally into the warmth of him, putting her arms around his neck.

'Time for bed, Scary,' he muttered, and she heard a catch in his voice. As he carried her through the villa to the bed-room in the back, Millie had the sleepy, hazy thought that there was nowhere else she'd rather be. In Chase's house. In Chase's arms. Going to Chase's bed.

CHAPTER SEVEN

MILLIE woke early, just as dawn was sliding its first pale fingers across the floor. She always woke early; quarter to five was usual. Yet, instead of bolting upright and practically sprinting to the shower, she woke slowly, languorously, stretching before she rolled over, propping herself up on one elbow to gaze at Chase.

He was fast asleep, his hair rumpled, his breathing slow and even. He looked gorgeous, and since he was asleep she let herself study him: the strong, stubbly angle of his jaw; the sweep of golden-brown lashes against his cheek. His lips were lush and full, his nose straight. The dawn light caught the golden glints in his close-cropped hair. Her gaze slid lower. He'd taken off his shirt. She'd seen his chest already, of course. He'd practically been shirtless the whole time she'd known him. Yet now she could study the perfect, muscled form; the sprinkling of dark-brown hair that veed lower, broad shoulders tapering to lean hips. The sheet was rucked about those hips, and she couldn't tell what he was wearing underneath. Dared she peek?

'Boxers, Scary.'

Her gaze flew back to his face. He was blinking sleep from his eyes and giving her the slowest, sexiest smile Millie had ever seen. Her heart juddered in her chest but she didn't try to dissemble.

'I was wondering. You seem like the type to sleep in the buff.'

'Nope, I'm strictly a boxers man. Sleeping naked can create all sorts of awkward situations, like when your cleaning lady arrives a bit earlier than you expected.'

Her mouth curved. 'You seem to have experienced a lot of awkward situations.'

'It certainly makes life a bit more interesting.'

'I'll take your word on it.'

He reached out and touched her hair, his fingers threading through it. 'Your hair's not so scary when you've slept on it.'

'It's probably a mess.'

'I like it.' He tucked a strand behind her ear, then trailed his fingers along her cheek before resting his thumb on the fullness of her lower lip. 'Those worry marks look a little better.'

'Do they?' Her heart had started the slow, thudding beat of expectation. They were both in a bed. Nearly naked. Had Chase removed her dress last night? She couldn't remember, but she was wearing one of his tee-shirts. And nothing underneath.

Surely now…?

'As enticing a prospect as that is, I think we'll have breakfast first,' Chase said, and Millie let out a huff of breath.

'Stop reading my mind.'

'It's too easy. Every thought is reflected in your eyes.'

'Not every thought,' Millie objected. She knew she had some secrets and she wanted to keep it that way.

Didn't she?

'More than you think,' Chase said softly, and he drew her towards him for a lingering kiss. It was the kind of kiss you had *after* you made love, slow and sated. It didn't have the urgency she expected, that she *felt*. Because today was day three of her week's holiday and since she'd met Chase time had started slipping by all too fast.

'Soon,' Chase murmured against her lips and she groaned. '*Stop* that.'

'Actually, I think you kind of like it.'

She didn't answer, because she knew he was right, even if the way he read her so easily was seriously annoying. She liked being *known*. 'What are we doing today?' she asked as she followed him out of the bedroom into the kitchen. Sunlight poured through the picture windows and Chase, still only wearing boxers, was reaching for the coffee grinder. Within seconds the wonderful aroma of freshly ground beans was wafting through the air.

'I thought you could decide that,' he said as he poured the ground beans into the coffee maker.

'Me?'

'Yes, you. You're not just along for the ride, you know.'

'I sort of thought I was. Your terms, remember?'

'Exactly. And my terms state that today you decide what we do. Of course, I have the right to veto any and all suggestions.'

'Oh, I see. Thanks for making that clear.'

'No problem.'

What *did* she want to do today? As Chase got out fresh melon and papaya and began slicing both, Millie considered. What did she want to do with *Chase*?

'I want to paint you.'

He paused, a mug in each hand, eyebrow arched. 'Too bad your paints are in the rubbish bin, then.'

'I can draw you,' Millie said firmly, surprised by how certain she felt. 'I brought charcoals too. They're in my suitcase.'

'So you've changed your mind about the painting thing?'

'Technically I won't be painting.'

'You are such a literalist.'

'Yes,' Millie said quietly, and it felt like a confession. 'I've changed my mind.'

Chase stared at her long and hard, and the moment unfurled, stretched between them into something that pulsed with both life and hope.

'OK,' he said. 'Breakfast, and then you can draw. I assume you'd prefer a nude model?'

She laughed and shook her head. 'You can keep your boxers on. For now.'

After a breakfast of coffee, fresh fruit and eggs Chase scrambled while Millie sat at the table and imagined just how she would sketch him, she fetched her paper and charcoals and they headed outside.

The day was warm, the sun already hot, although a fresh breeze blew off the sea. Millie had changed into a polo shirt and capris, and Chase had, on her instruction, put on a tee-shirt and shorts.

'Are you sure you don't want me nude?' he said, sounding disappointed, and Millie shook her head.

'Far too distracting.'

'Well, that's something at least.'

'Just try to act natural.'

He gave an exaggerated sigh. 'Whenever someone says that, you can't act natural any more.'

'Try.'

'I bet you're a real ball-breaker at work.'

'That,' Millie informed him, 'is a horrible, sexist term.'

'But you are, right?' He positioned himself on the sand, hands stretched out behind him, legs in front. 'This OK?'

'Perfect.' She found a comfortable spot just a little bit away and laid the sketch pad across her knees. After staring at Chase this morning, she realised how much she wanted to draw him, to capture the ease and joy of his body and face so she could remember it always.

So she could have something of him even when this week was over.

She swallowed, also realising just how much she was starting to care for him. Forty-eight hours—forty-eight *intense* hours—were changing how she felt. Changing *her*.

'You going to put pencil to paper this time, Scary?'

'Yes.' Swallowing, she looked down at her paper, began to roughly sketch the shape of him.

'So you haven't been doing the art thing for a while,' Chase remarked, gazing out to the sea so she should capture his profile. 'Why did you stop?'

Millie hesitated. She knew she should remind him about the no-talking rule, but it seemed kind of pointless to keep at it now. She didn't even want to. She could still control what she told him. 'Life happened,' she said. 'I got too busy and drawing seemed kind of a silly pastime.' And totally out of sync with her and Rob's focused, career-driven lives.

'And then you finally took a holiday and thought you might like to try again?'

'Basically.'

'So why did you throw out the paints when I first met you?'

'All these questions,' Millie said lightly. 'You are *so* violating our agreement, Chase.'

'But you're answering them,' he pointed out. 'For once.'

She didn't speak for a moment, just sketched faster and faster, the feel and look of him emerging from her charcoal. 'I didn't like how obvious it seemed,' she finally said. 'Like I was trying to *find* myself or something.'

'Were you?'

She glanced up, the sketch book momentarily forgotten. 'I'm not lost,' she said sharply. 'I'm not *broken*.'

'You're not?' He still spoke mildly, yet she felt that spurt of rage anyway. Her fingers tightened around the charcoal.

'No.'

'Because I think you are.'

Shock had her fingers slackening again, and the charcoal fell to the ground. 'How dare—?'

'Why do you think you're here, Millie?' He turned to gaze at her and she saw a blaze of emotion lighting his eyes. 'Why do you think you were willing to have this crazy, intense week? And not just willing, but needing it?'

'I don't *need* it.'

'Liar.'

She shook her head, hating that he saw through her. Hating that she didn't have the strength to deny it any longer. She *was* lost. Broken. And she needed this week with him; she needed *him*.

And he knew it.

He kept his gaze on her, assessing, knowing, and she hated that too. The raw honesty between them in this moment felt more exposing and intimate than lying naked on a bed with him had yesterday.

She reached for the dropped charcoal, her fingers closing around it even though she knew she wouldn't draw any more. She couldn't. She stared blindly at the sketch pad, her mind spinning, her heart thudding.

'Our session is finished, I presume?' Chase drawled, and Millie nodded jerkily. 'And now you're going to go all haughty on me, aren't you? The Millie Lang armour goes up, and you get all scary and severe.'

'You're the one who calls me scary,' Millie said through numb lips. Every instinct in her was telling her to *run*. Save herself, or as much of herself as she could. How had she let it get this far? Chase had been so clever at seducing her into an emotional intimacy she had never intended to give or reveal. Damn it, all she'd wanted was *sex*.

And they still hadn't had it.

Maybe it was time to rectify that situation.

'I'm not going to go scary on you,' she told him, clutching her sketch pad to her chest. 'But you did say I could decide what we did today, and now I've decided.'

'And it's not sketching?' Chase still looked relaxed, still had his hands stretched out behind him like he was enjoying a nice morning in the sun.

'No, it's not.' Her voice still rang out, strident, aggressive. It sounded strong, even if she didn't feel it. 'I'll tell you what it is.'

'I bet I could guess…' Chase murmured and, furious that he still seemed to know her so well, she cut across him.

'It's sex. I want to have sex with you.'

Chase regarded her with lazy amusement, although he was far from feeling either lazy or amused. He knew Millie felt vulnerable and exposed, but damn it so did he. He hadn't meant to say any of that. Lost? Broken? He could have been talking about himself. What the hell had he been thinking, getting that honest? That *real*?

He hadn't been thinking at all. He'd just been acting on instinct, allowing the deep within him to call to the deep within her. And for a few charged seconds he knew they'd connected in a way that was far more powerful than anything they could do on a bed—or whatever surface they chose.

'You want to have sex with me,' Chase repeated. 'Sometimes, Millie, you have a one-track mind.'

'I'm serious, Chase. The whole reason we're having this stupid fling is—'

'Now our fling is stupid? I'm offended.'

'You know what I mean. I started this because—'

'*You* started it?'

'Stop interrupting me!'

'Because I'm the one who walked up to you on that beach, sweetheart. *And* asked you out.'

'I'm the one who suggested we sleep together.'

'I'll concede that point, but that's the only shot you're going to call.'

She stared at him, her face white, her lips bloodless. What had scared her so much? The fact that he saw her need, or that she sensed his own? And how did she think sex was going to solve anything?

On second thought...

'OK, Scary.' Chase rose from the beach, turning his face so Millie didn't see him grimace at the throbbing ache of his joints. It was getting worse. The new medication wasn't helping as much as he'd hoped. Hell, he was as broken as she was. He just hid it better.

'OK?' she repeated uncertainly, the wind blowing her hair into tangles even as she clutched the sketch pad to her chest like it was a body shield.

'OK, we'll have sex. I think we've had a fair amount of anticipation, don't you?'

'Yes.' She sounded uncertain. He wasn't surprised. She hadn't expected him to agree—well, guess what? Sex was probably the only place where he could make her let go of that all-too-precious control. Break the barriers she surrounded herself with, force her to be exposed and empty; only then could she be covered and filled.

Is that what you really want?

Yes. Certainty blazed through him, surprising him. He didn't know more than that, wouldn't look farther. *No more questions.*

Time to act.

'Come on,' he said, and reached a hand down to her. She

took it gingerly, her eyes so heartbreakingly wide, her teeth sunk deep into her lower lip.

'Where are we going?'

'I told you I prefer to make love on a bed, right?'

'Yes…'

'Cold feet?' he jibed softly, knowing she'd rise to that easy bait.

'No! Of course not!'

'Of course not,' he agreed. Yet her hand was icy-cold and her slender fingers felt like bird bones in his.

He led her back inside, through the house and then right to his bedroom door. Turned to her as he still held that icy, trembling hand. 'You're scared.'

She opened her mouth to deny it, then stopped. 'Yes.'

'You're thinking too much.'

'I know.'

'I think,' Chase murmured, 'I know a way to make you to stop thinking.' He kicked open the door and pulled her into the bedroom.

Millie felt weirdly numb as she followed Chase into the bedroom. It looked the same as it had a few hours earlier, when they'd lain in that nice, wide bed and talked and teased each other.

It *felt* totally different now.

Her heart was thudding so hard it hurt. Her mouth was dry. Her legs felt like jelly. She didn't think she'd ever felt this nervous before. Fizzing with both fear and a glorious anticipation. She wanted this, even if it scared her senseless.

Chase turned to her, his expression serious. Thoughtful. She closed her eyes and tipped her head back, waited for him to take over. Make her stop thinking.

He didn't do anything. She opened her eyes. 'What are you waiting for?'

He smiled. 'Sorry, Scary, this isn't the Chase Bryant Show.'

'You want me to do something?'

'I know you'd rather I just did everything, but since when have I ever let you have it easy?'

She let out a trembling huff of laughter. 'Sorry. It's... It's been a long time.'

'I kind of figured that out.'

She closed her eyes again, this time in embarrassment. With her eyes closed, she couldn't see him but she felt him step closer, felt the whisper of his fingers as he brushed her cheek, tucked her hair behind her ear. 'Telling you to relax isn't going to do a thing, is it?' She shook her head, felt Chase's hesitation. 'You sure you want to do this, Millie? You know you could back out now. I wouldn't— Well, yeah, I'd mind, but I'd understand. This is big for you. And scary. I get that.'

A hot lump of emotion lodged in her throat. Speaking was impossible. She just shook her head, eyes still closed. She heard Chase's soft breathing, felt his fingers gently brush her cheek again.

Finally she opened her eyes. He looked so concerned and tender as he gazed down at her that her heart seemed to seize up. Her emotions were fully engaged, much more than she'd ever intended or wanted. And, even though it terrified her, she knew bone-deep that she really *did* want this. She craved it. Not just the physical release, but the emotional intensity. *Intimacy.* How scary was that?

'I might not be doing much,' she whispered, 'but I'm not trying to leave, am I?'

'No. You're not. And thank God for that.' Slowly, deliberately, he drew her towards him, his hands cradling her face. Her heart pounded. This was it. He was going to kiss her, and then...

'Stop *thinking*, Scary.'

'I can't help it,' she groaned. 'I can't turn my mind off.'

'I realise.'

'I want to turn it off, Chase. I want to forget. I want to forget everything.' Her mouth was a whisper away from his. He gazed down at her, his eyes warm and soft with compassion as his thumbs stroked her jaw bone.

'But then you'll just have to remember again.'

'Just for a little while. I want to forget for a little while.' She drew in a shaky breath. 'Please. Make me forget. Make me forget everything.'

He smiled faintly even though she saw a shadow of concern in his eyes. 'That's kind of a tall order.'

'You're the only one who can.' And she knew she spoke the truth. '*Please*. Whatever it takes.'

In answer he kissed her, his lips brushing hers once, twice, as if getting the sense of her before he suddenly delved deep and she felt that kiss straight down to her soul. Shocks of pleasure and excitement sizzled along her nerve endings and she surrendered to that kiss, kissing him back, hands curling around his shoulders, nails digging in.

Yet even as she surrendered her mind took a step back. She started thinking. It was as if that kiss had taken over every part of her body and mind except that one dark corner where the memories crouched, waited till she was vulnerable to attack.

You never kissed Rob like this.

You shouted at him before he left for the last time.

You didn't kiss Charlotte goodbye. You didn't even look at her.

'*Easy*, Millie.' She opened her eyes and realised she'd been standing rigid, her nails like claws in Chase's shoulders.

'I'm sorry.'

'So am I.' Gently he unhooked her hands from his shoulders. 'You were doing some serious thinking there.' Chase stared at her for a moment, and then he took her by the hand and led her to the bed. He stripped off his shirt and dropped his shorts. Millie blinked. She'd seen him naked yesterday, but he was still magnificent. Beautiful, everything taut and sculpted and golden-brown.

'Now I'm naked,' he said.

'Clearly.'

'You still have your clothes on.'

'I'm aware.'

'I'm going to take them off.'

Her heart turned over. 'OK,' she said. He'd seen her naked yesterday, but that had been her choice. Her action. Now, as she stood still and he reached for the buttons on her shirt, she knew it was his. She'd just relinquished a little bit of control, just as he wanted her to. As she wanted to, even if it was so incredibly hard.

Deftly Chase's fingers undid the buttons on her polo shirt. 'Raise your arms,' he said, and she did. He slipped the shirt over her head, tossed it aside. Millie glanced down at the plain white cotton bra she wore; the straps were frayed. *Why* had she never indulged in sexy underwear? 'We'll leave that on for now,' Chase said, his mouth quirking in a small smile. 'I kind of like it.'

She practically snorted in disbelief. 'You like my old, plain white bra?'

'I know; weird, huh? But I've seen plenty of push-up monstrosities. This doesn't pretend or hide.' He touched her chin, tilting her face so she had to meet his gaze. 'Unlike you.'

'My *bra* is more honest than I am?' she huffed.

'Pretty much,' he said, and undid the snap on her capris.

Millie's breath caught in her chest as Chase slid them down her legs. His touch was feather-light and swift, hardly a practised caress. And yet she felt as if she burned where his fingers had so briefly touched her. He sank to his knees as he balanced her with one hand while he used the other to help her out of the capris, then tossed them over with the shirt.

She was in her underwear. Again.

And he was naked, on his knees in front of her.

She tried not to gulp too loudly as she gazed down at him, all burnished, sleek muscle. Slowly, so slowly, he slid his hands up her legs and then held her by the hips, his palms seeming to burn right through the thin cotton of her underwear as his fingers slid over her butt. She let out a stifled cry as he brought his mouth close to the juncture of her thighs and she tensed, anticipating his touch, fearing the intensity of her own response. But he didn't touch her, just let his breath fan over her, and that was enough.

Her knees buckled.

She *felt* Chase's smile and he stood up. 'Better,' he said, and she let out a wobbly laugh. Sensation fizzed inside her. The fear lessened, replaced by a warm, honeyed desire.

Then her mind started going into hyperdrive again, memories, thoughts and fears tumbling around like a washer on spin cycle.

'Stop thinking.'

'I *can't*.'

'Then I'll have to help you.'

'Yes.' *Please*.

Wordlessly he tugged her hand and led her to the bed. Her mind was still spinning relentlessly, and she had a sudden picture of her bed back in New York, her and Rob's bed, all hospital corners and starched duvet, and how she'd sank onto it when the phone had rung, and the police had told her there had been an accident…

'Lie down.'

'OK.' She felt only relief that he was interrupting her thoughts. She wanted to stop thinking. Stop analysing. Stop remembering so much. Why did being with Chase make her remember? She'd spent two years trying *not* to think, and now the thoughts came fast and thick, unstoppable.

She needed Chase to stop them.

She lay on the bed and he knelt over her. Millie felt herself tense. 'What are you—?'

'Trust me.'

And she knew she did trust him. Amazingly. Implicitly. Yet that thought was scary too. Chase reached for something above her head, and she saw he'd taken the satin pillow-case from the pillow.

He took the pillow-case off the other pillow and Millie waited, arousal and uncertainty warring within her.

'Care to tell me what's going on?' she asked as lightly as she could.

Chase slowly slid his hand from her shoulder to her palm, lacing her fingers with his own as he raised her hand above her head.

'I'm tying you up.'

'What?' She thought he was joking. Of course he was joking. Then she realised he'd done it, and her hand was tied to the bed post with a satin pillow-case. She stared at him with wide eyes, totally shocked. Chase simply knelt there, smiling faintly, his eyes dark and serious. Waiting.

Waiting for her permission.

She drew in a deep, shuddering breath, her whole body intensely, unbearably aware. She had no room for thoughts. She said nothing.

He bent down and kissed her deeply on the mouth, another soul-stirring kiss that had her arching instinctively towards him.

And then he tied up her other hand. She lay there, her hands tied above her head, her body completely open to his caress.

Vulnerable.

This felt far more intense than anything that had happened so far between them, and she knew why Chase was doing it.

He was taking everything from her. Taking it all, so he could give.

All in.

Slowly Chase slid his hands across her tummy, over her breasts, reaching behind to unhook her bra. 'Sorry,' he whispered. 'I do like it, but it had to go eventually.'

She still couldn't speak. Especially not when he tossed the bra onto the floor and bent his head to her breasts, his tongue flicking lightly over her nipples. She arched again, her head thrown back, pleasure streaking through her like lightning—but still the thoughts.

My breasts are too small.

Rob never liked them.

I don't deserve a man like this.

'Still thinking, huh?' He lifted his head and looked at her, his voice wry even as his eyes blazed.

'Sorry,' she whispered. She wanted him to help her forget, but maybe she couldn't forget unless she first released the memories. *Shared* them.

The most terrifying thought of all.

'Don't be sorry.'

'I want to stop thinking so much. Remembering.'

'I know you do.'

'Help me,' she implored. 'Help me, Chase.'

He gazed at her, his face suffused with both tenderness and desire. What a heady combination. She felt more for him in that moment then she ever had before, and then he took another pillow-case, folded it in half and placed it over her eyes. Millie gasped aloud. Chase waited, the pillow-case folded over her eyes but not tied.

She blinked, shocked and yet knowing she needed this.

Chase was helping her, helping her in a way she'd never have expected. It was strange and scary, yet amazingly *right*.

'OK?' he asked softly and she nodded. He tied the blindfold around her eyes.

Millie lay there, trying to adjust to this new reality. Her world had shrunk to the feel, sound and scent of Chase. Her mind had no room save for the sense of him. Her body tensed in a kind of exquisite anticipation, waiting for his touch. Wondering where he would touch her, every nerve taut with glorious expectation as she lay there, helpless, *hopeful* and utterly in his control.

And then she felt his mouth between her thighs, right on the centre of her, and she let out a shudder of shocked pleasure. She had not expected *that*.

Her body writhed beneath him and she felt a pleasure so intense it was akin to pain as her body surged towards a climax. '*Chase*,' she gasped, his name a sob. And then he stopped, taking her to the brink and no further, and she ached with the loss of him. 'Chase,' she said again, and this time it was a plea.

She could hear his breathing, ragged and uneven, and his knees pressed on the outside of her thighs. She felt his heat, knew he was right above her. Where would he touch her next?

She let out a long shudder, every sense sizzling with excitement.

And then he began to touch her, a blitz of caresses that had her so focused on the sensation she could not form so much as a single coherent thought. First a butterfly brush of a kiss on her wrist. A blizzard of kisses on her throat. Then he kissed her deeply on the mouth and she responded, straining against the bonds that had brought her to this moment. He kissed her everywhere, light, teasing kisses, deep-throated demands, bites, licks and nibbles. She cried beneath him, first out of pleasure and amazement and then something deeper.

Something inside her started to break.

She'd told him she wasn't broken, and she hadn't been. She'd been holding herself together, only just, her soul and heart a maze of hairline cracks and fissures. And now, under Chase, she shattered.

Pain and pleasure, joy and sorrow, erupted from the depths of her being in helpless cries that became wrenching sobs, her whole body shaking with the force of them even as she lay there, splayed open to him, everything exposed. Everything vulnerable.

'Millie,' he said, and his voice was full of love.

'Yes,' she choked. 'Yes, Chase, *now.*'

Distantly she heard the rip of foil and knew Chase would finally be inside her. She'd never wanted anything so much, and yet she still gave a cry of surprise and joy when she felt him slide inside, fill her up.

She'd been so *empty.*

His arms came around her and Chase freed her so she enfolded her body around his, drawing him deeper inside as she buried her face in his neck and sobbed through her climax.

Chase surged inside her, deeper and deeper, and with his arms around her, holding her tightly and tenderly to him, he brought them both home.

CHAPTER EIGHT

CHASE felt his heart race as he held Millie in his arms and she sobbed as if her own heart were breaking.

God help him. God help them both. He'd never expected sex between them to be like *that*. Mind-blowing indeed. He was completely and utterly spent, emotionally, physically, everything.

Millie pressed her face against his neck, her body shaking with the force of her emotion. Chase didn't speak, knew there were no words. He just stroked her back, her hair, wiped the tears from her cheeks with his thumbs.

Millie's sobs began to subside into snuffles and hiccups, and she curled herself into him, as if she wanted to be as close to him as possible, her legs across his, her arm around his waist, her head still buried against his neck.

Chase held her, cradled her closer, even as part of him was distantly acknowledging that this had been one *hell* of a mistake.

She lifted her face from his neck and gazed up at him with rain-washed eyes. She looked so unbearably open; she'd dropped all the armour and masks. Nothing hid her from him any more, and he really wasn't sure how he felt about that. He shifted so he could hold her a bit more loosely, waiting for her to speak.

'I want to tell you,' she said quietly, hesitantly. 'I want to—to talk about my past.'

He didn't think he wanted to hear it. Chase adjusted her more securely against him, knowing she needed that. She needed him, God help them both.

'OK,' he said.

Millie glanced down, ran her hand down the length of his bare chest. Even now he reacted, felt the shower of sparks her touch created in him. He wanted to dismiss it as mere chemistry, but he knew he couldn't.

'My husband died two years ago,' Millie said, and everything, *everything* in him shrivelled.

Damn.

'I'm sorry,' he said quietly. He'd suspected some heartbreak; of course he had. How could he not? Sadness seeped from her pores. But a husband? A *widow*? He thought of all his light, deprecating jokes and inwardly winced.

Outwardly he ran his hand up and down her back, strokes meant to soothe and comfort even as his mind seethed.

'What happened?' he asked eventually, because for all her wanting to tell him everything she'd lapsed into silence.

'He died in a car accident. On the Cross Bronx expressway. A collision with an eighteen-wheeler. They think the driver fell asleep at the wheel.'

Chase swallowed. He couldn't think of anything more to say, so he just held her.

'I didn't tell you because for the last two years it's completely defined me. Everyone I know looks at me like I'm a walking tragedy.' Which she was. 'No one knows what to say to me, so they either ignore me or apologise. I hate it.'

He identified all too much with everything she said, albeit for a different reason. But he knew there was more she wasn't telling him.

'And then I feel guilty for thinking that way. Like I want to be happy, even when I know I never can be.'

'Everyone wants to be happy,' Chase said. 'You can be happy again, Millie.' But not with him. Now, he knew, was not the time to remind her they only had one week together. Four more days after this.

'I liked the fact that you didn't know,' she said quietly. 'That you treated me normally. I almost—I almost felt normal.'

'And then you felt guilty for feeling normal,' Chase supplied. What a depressing cycle.

'Yes, I suppose,' Millie said slowly. 'But more than that.' She stopped again and he knew he would have to prompt her. Coax the heartbreaking story with all its drama and tragedy out of her bit by bit.

But he didn't think he had the energy. That probably made him an incredibly shallow bastard, but he couldn't help it. He'd had his own share of depressing drama, tragedy and pain. He wasn't sure he could take Millie's.

And he knew she couldn't take his.

'We had a good marriage,' she finally said. 'I loved him.' And what was he supposed to say to *that*? She bowed her head, her hair brushing his bare chest. 'And I know no marriage, no relationship is perfect, but I look back and I see all the mistakes I made. We both made,' she allowed, her voice a throaty whisper, and Chase just let her talk. He didn't have much to offer her. He hadn't had too many serious relationships, and he'd never come close to marriage.

Yet.

Why the *hell* had he thought that?

'We grew apart,' Millie said after a moment. 'Because… because of different things. And the day he died I was sharp with him. I don't even remember what we argued about, isn't that stupid? But I didn't— I didn't kiss them—

him—goodbye. I don't think I even *said* goodbye. And Charlotte...' Her voice caught and Chase pulled her closer. He still didn't say anything. He had nothing to offer her in this moment, and he knew it. Maybe she did too.

After a ragged moment Millie slipped from his arms. He let her go, watched from the bed as she scooped up her clothes and headed towards the bathroom. 'I'm going to take a shower,' she said, her back to him so he could see all the delicate knobs of her spine, the slender dip of her waist and curve of her hip.

'OK,' Chase said, and as she closed the bathroom door he felt a shaming wave of relief.

Millie turned the knobs on the shower and rested her head on the cool tile. Her heart had stopped its thunderous racing and for a second she wondered if it still beat at all. After feeling so painfully, gloriously alive, she now felt dead inside. Numb and lifeless with disappointment.

So Chase didn't really want intense. Not the kind of intense she'd been offering as she'd lain in his arms and tried to tell him her story. Even as he put his arms around her, went through the motions, she'd felt the coldness of his emotional withdrawal. She'd violated the terms of their agreement— the terms *she* had made—and he didn't like it. Didn't want to go that deep or far.

Stupid, *stupid* her.

Drawing a shaky breath, she stepped into the shower, let the water stream over her and wash away the traces of her tears. She'd cried after the accident, of course. She'd done the counselling and the support groups and even *journalled*. But she'd never cried like that. She'd never given so much, so freely, and stupidly it made her want more. It made her want to tell him everything, about her marriage, the accident, *Charlotte*.

But within thirty seconds of speaking she'd realised Chase didn't want to know. He wasn't the only one who could read people.

Another shuddering breath and she reached for the shampoo. At least now she understood the terms: no talking about the past. Chase was all about the physical intimacy, having her melt in his arms, but the emotional stuff? Not so much. He'd liked pushing her but he didn't like the results. Well, she got that now. And it was just as well, because even if for a few shattering seconds she'd wanted to tell him everything, had maybe even thought she *loved* him, she understood now that wasn't where this was going. And when rationality had returned she'd known she didn't even want to go there. She'd loved and lost once. She wasn't going to attempt it again, and especially not with a man who was only in it for a week.

By the time she'd showered and dressed, Millie felt more herself. She'd found that icy control, and she was glad. She stepped out of the bathroom, saw the late-afternoon sun slant across the empty bed. They'd skipped lunch and, despite the emotional tornado she'd been sucked into all afternoon, she was hungry. Her stomach growled.

She wandered out to the kitchen and saw Chase talking on his mobile. She waited, far enough way so she couldn't eavesdrop, and a few seconds later he disconnected the call and gave her a quick, breezy smile.

'Good shower?'

'Fine. I'm starving, though.'

'I'm glad to hear it. I just made reservations at Straw Hat on Anguilla.'

'Anguilla? How far away is that?'

'An hour in my boat.'

'OK.' Maybe escaping the island would be a good thing. The door bell rang, and Millie watched as Chase went to answer it. She felt like everything was on fast forward, plans put in motion before she could even think.

'What's that?' she asked when he came back with several shopping bags with the resort's swirly logo on the side.

'A couple of dresses. I thought you might like something new.'

She gazed at him levelly. 'I have a whole suitcase of new clothes.'

Chase just shrugged. 'I don't think your wardrobe runs to fun and flirty.'

'Maybe I don't want *fun and flirty.*'

He sighed. 'Don't wear them if you don't want to, Millie. I just thought it might be nice for our big date.'

'Oh? So this is a big date?'

He narrowed his gaze. 'What's with you?'

'Nothing.' Somehow everything had changed between them, and not for the better. Chase wasn't as light and laughing as he'd used to be, as she *needed* him to be. He was tense and touchy, even if he was trying to act like he wasn't. And so was she.

'Fine. I'll take a look.' She reached for the bags and caught Chase's bemused look. 'Thank you,' she added, belatedly and ungraciously.

Chase's mouth quirked in a smile that seemed all too sad. 'No problem,' he said quietly, and she retreated to the bedroom.

Half an hour later she was on Chase's boat, wearing a shift dress of cinnamon-coloured silk as they cruised towards Anguilla.

Chase had shed his blazer and tie and rolled the sleeves up of his crisp white shirt to navigate the boat. He looked amazing.

They hadn't said much since the exchange in the kitchen, and the silence was making Millie twitchy. She wanted that fun, teasing banter back, the ease she'd felt in Chase's presence. She'd told him he'd made her uncomfortable, but it was nothing like this.

Moodily she stared out at the sea. The sun was already slipping towards the horizon. A third sunset. Only four more to go and their week would be over. And by mutual agreement, they would never see each other again.

Chase left the tiller to come and sit next to her, the wind ruffling his hair as he squinted into the dying sun. He didn't ask her what she was thinking, didn't say anything, and Millie knew he didn't want to know. He'd only pushed her when he thought she'd push back, not give in. It was the anticipation that had been fun for him, the moment before.

Not the moment after.

'So how come you have a villa on St Julian's if you didn't want to have anything to do with the Bryant business?' she asked when the silence had stretched on long enough to make her want to fidget.

Chase kept his gaze on the darkening sea. 'My grandfather bequeathed the island to my brothers and me, and my father couldn't do anything about it. As soon as I'd established myself I had the villa built. I hardly ever use it, actually, but it was a way to thumb my nose at my father—even if he was dead.'

'It must have hurt, to have him disinherit you,' Millie said quietly.

Chase shrugged. 'It didn't feel good.'

'What about your mother?'

'She died when I was twelve. Breast cancer.'

'I'm sorry.'

Another shrug. Clearly he didn't like talking about any of this, but at least he was giving answers. And Millie knew she wanted to know.

'And your brothers? Do you get along well with them?'

He sighed, raked a hand through his hair. 'More or less. Aaron is nice enough, but he views life as a game of Monopoly where he has all the money. Luke is my middle brother, and he's always been trying to prove himself. Total workaholic.'

'And where do you fit in?'

'Black sheep, basically, who only semi-made-good.'

'Are they married?'

'Nope, none of us seem eager to take the plunge.' He spoke evenly, almost lightly, but she still heard the warning. *Oh, fabulous.* So after this afternoon he thought she was going to go all doe-eyed on him, start dreaming of happily-ever-afters. She'd only done that for a *second.*

'And you get along?'

'More or less.'

It didn't sound like the best family situation. She was blessed to have parents and a sister who loved and supported her, but even they hadn't been able to break down her walls or keep her from hiding behind the rubble.

Only Chase had done that.

She let out a restless sigh, knowing she needed to stop thinking this way, wanting something from Chase he couldn't give. Ironic, really, that she'd assumed he was shallow, then believed he wasn't, only to discover he really was. And, while she'd wanted shallow before, she didn't want it now.

'And what about you? You have family around?' Chase asked.

'Parents and a sister.'

'Are you close with them?'

'Yes.' She paused, because even though she was close she hadn't told them as much about her marriage as she had Chase.

'Not that close, huh?' Chase said, sounding cynical, and

Millie shook her head. She couldn't bear for him to think that her family was like his, or that her life had been all sadness.

'No, actually, we are. My sister Zoe is fantastic. She stops by almost every week with my favourite snack, makes sure I'm not working too hard.'

'Your favourite snack?'

'Nachos with fake cheese.'

He let a short laugh. 'That is so low-brow. I was expecting dark chocolate or some exotic sorbet.'

'I don't play to type *that* much,' she said lightly, and for a moment everything was at it had been, the lightness, the fun. Then something shuttered in Chase's eyes and he turned away to gaze at the sea.

'We're almost there.' He rose and went to trim the sail as the lights of Anguilla loomed closer, shimmering on the surface of the tranquil sun-washed sea. They didn't speak as he moored the boat and then helped her onto the dock.

The restaurant was right on the sand, the terracotta-tile and white-stucco building one of a jumble along the beach. It felt surprisingly refreshing to be out of the rarefied atmosphere of St Julian's, to see people who weren't just wealthy guests. A rail-thin cat perched along the wall that lined the beach, and a few children played with a ball and stick in the dusky light.

Millie slowed her steps as she watched the children. One of the girls had a mop of dark curls. She looked to be about five years old, a little older than Charlotte would have been.

'Millie?' Chase reached for her hand and she realised she'd been just standing there, staring. Children had been invisible to her for two years; it was as if her brain knew she couldn't handle it and just blanked them out. She didn't see them in her building, in the street, in the park. It helped that her life was so work-focused; there weren't many children on Wall Street.

Yet she saw them now, saw them in all their round-cheeked innocence, and felt her raw and wounded heart give a death-defying squeeze.

'Millie,' Chase said again quietly and slowly she turned away from the raggedy little group. She wanted to rail at him, to beat her fists against his chest.

See? See what you did to me? I was fine before, I was surviving, and now you've opened up this need and hope in me and you don't even want it any more.

Swallowing, she lifted her chin and followed Chase into the restaurant. The place was a mix of funky Caribbean decor and fresh, well-prepared food. The waiter greeted Chase by name and ushered them to the best table in the restaurant, in a semi-secluded alcove.

'What's this? A huge ashtray?' Millie gestured to the rectangular box of sand in the middle of the table.

'Nope, just a little sand box to play with while we wait for our food.' He took a little spade lying next to the box and handed it to her with a glinting smile. 'Dig in.'

'Clearly meant for guests with short attention spans.' She scooped a bit of sand with the miniature spade and dumped it out again. 'So do you like being an architect?'

'All these questions.'

She glanced up sharply. 'It's called conversation, generally.' She heard an edge to her voice, knew he heard it too. So *now* he didn't like the questions.

Chase leaned back in his chair and took a sip of sparkling water. 'I like making things. I like having an idea and seeing it become a reality.'

'What firm do you work for?'

His mouth quirked upwards. 'Chase Bryant Designs.'

'Your own.'

'Yep, started it five years ago.' He spoke casually, but she heard a betraying note of pride in his voice. He'd made something of himself, and without help from his wealthy family. She wanted to tell him she admired that, that she was proud of him, but how stupid would that be? He'd just feel even more awkward. So she took a large gulp of wine, and then another, deciding that alcohol was a better option.

'Slow down there, Scary,' Chase said, eyeing her near-empty wine glass. 'Or I'll have to carry you home.'

'I'm not a lightweight.'

'No, indeed.' Now she heard an edge in his voice, and she pushed her wine glass away with a little sigh of irritation.

'Look, Chase, why don't you just come out and say it?'

He stilled. Stared. 'Say what?'

'You're done.'

'*I'm* done?'

'Yes. Ever since—' She paused, swallowed. 'It's obvious you've had your bout of intense sex and you're ready to move on. So maybe we should call it a day. A night. Whatever.' She grabbed her wine glass again and drained it, half-wishing she hadn't started this conversation.

Half-wishing even now he'd tell her she was wrong.

'You're the one who has been picking fights,' Chase said mildly. 'I bought you a dress and took you out to one of the best restaurants in the whole Caribbean. So, sorry, I don't get where you're coming from.'

She met his gaze squarely. 'You don't?' she asked quietly, no edge, no spite. Just raw honesty.

Chase held her gaze for a breathless beat and then glanced away. 'No, I don't,' he said quietly, and she felt that tiny tendril of hope she'd still been nurturing even without knowing it shrivel and die.

It hurt that, after all they'd experienced and shared, he wouldn't even own up to how things had changed. It hurt far too much.

She'd known this man for three days. Yet time had lost its

meaning in this surprising paradise; time had lost its meaning ever since she'd agreed to have this fling—this intense, intimate, all-in fling—with Chase.

For a second Millie almost rose from the table and walked out of the restaurant. She didn't need this. She didn't need Chase. Then the waiter came and they gave their orders, and the impulse passed, her strength fading away.

For it was weakness why she stayed. A weakness for him. That little tendril of hope might have withered and died, but its seed still remained in the stubborn soil of her heart, desperate to grow.

Chase watched the emotions—disappointment, hurt, sorrow—ripple across Millie's face like shadows on water, wishing he couldn't read her so easily. Wishing he wasn't screwing up so badly right now.

Nothing had been the same since the sex, and more importantly since the conversation after the sex. He'd pushed and pushed Millie, had wanted to see her lose that control, had wanted to be the one to make it happen. And when it had, and she'd taken a flying leap over that cliff, what had he done?

He'd backed away, and pretended he hadn't. Acted like he was still right there with her, flying through the air, when she knew he'd really high-tailed it in the other direction.

Coward. *Bastard.*

He took a sip of water and stared moodily around at the restaurant. He'd always enjoyed this place, found it fun and relaxing, but not this time. Now he didn't think anything would kick-start his mood. He wanted the fun back with Millie, the easy companionship they'd had. He hadn't even realised just how easy it had been, until now.

Now words tangled in his throat and he couldn't get any of it out. Couldn't even begin. What to say? *I'm sorry. I'm sorry I'm not there for you, when you thought I would be. When you wanted me to be and I just couldn't do it.*

Hell, this was all his fault. He should have listened to that cool, rational part of his brain that had told him to walk away from this woman before she drove him insane. Who said no to 'intense', no to a fling, no to anything with Millie Lang.

Instead he'd done the opposite, followed his libido and even his heart, and now he had no idea what to do. He hated seeing the deepening frown lines on Millie's face, the worry marks on her lip fresher and more raw than ever. As he watched a little bright-red pearl of blood appeared on her lower lip from where she'd bitten it.

Damn. Damn it to hell.

'Millie…' He reached over, placed his hand on hers. She looked up, eyes wide, teeth sunk into that lip. 'I'm sorry,' he said in a low voice. 'I've totally screwed this up.'

Tears filled those soft brown eyes and she blinked hard as she shook her head, teeth biting even deeper. 'No. I'm the one who screwed up. I shouldn't have said all that…after. That wasn't part of our deal.'

'I led you to it.'

She arched an eyebrow, somehow managed a smile. This woman was *strong*. 'By tying me up and blindfolding me?'

'Basically.'

'Have you ever done that kind of thing before?' she asked, curious, and he actually blushed.

'No.'

'Me neither.'

'Yeah, I pretty much figured that out.'

She let out a laugh that trembled just a little too much. 'Oh, Chase, I just want it back.'

He eyed her warily. 'Back?'

'You. Me. *Us*. I was having fun, you know, and that felt

really good.' She gave him a wobbly smile that felt like a dagger thrust to the heart. 'It felt amazing.'

And he knew she was right. It *had* felt amazing. More amazing than anything else he'd ever had or known. Why was he pushing it away?

Four more days.

'Come on,' he said roughly. He rose from the table, nearly knocking over their drinks as he threw down some bills. 'Let's get out of here.'

She rose also, taking his hand as he threaded his way through the table. 'Where are we going?'

'To a room. A room with a bed.'

'Or any convenient surface?' she murmured, and something close to fierce joy pulsed through him.

'That's about the size of it,' he agreed, and led her out into the night.

Millie didn't ask questions, didn't say anything at all as he led her away from the beach and towards the street. He hailed a cab, thanked God one screeched to the kerb in three seconds flat and then hauled her inside it.

Still no speaking. Would words break what was between them? Chase didn't know. Was afraid to find out. And yet he had words, so many words, words he needed to say and, more importantly, she needed to hear.

But, first, a room. A bed.

'Cap Juluca,' he told the cab driver, and Millie just arched an eyebrow. 'It's a resort here,' Chase explained, his voice still rough with want. 'I booked it in case we didn't feel like sailing back.'

And that was all that was said as they drove away from Meads Bay, down the coast, through the resort's gates, and then up to the main building. Chase kept hold of her hand as he checked in and then led her away from the main complex towards the private cove that housed their accommodation.

Millie skidded to a stop. 'A grass hut? Seriously?'

'A luxurious grass hut,' Chase said and tugged her inside.

Millie glanced around and he could see her taking in the polished mahogany floor, the comfortable rattan chairs, the gauzy mosquito netting. And the bed. A wide, low bed with linen sheets and soft pillows, the ocean lapping only metres away through the draped net curtains. The wind rustled through the woven grass that made up the roof and walls.

She turned to him. 'It's beautiful.'

'You're beautiful,' he said, a catch in his voice, and she shook her head.

'I don't need flattery, Chase. I know I'm not beautiful.' She sounded so matter-of-fact, it made his heart twist inside him.

'Why do you think you aren't beautiful?'

'Even you called me scary. And I know I'm not your usual type.' She let out a long, low breath. 'Look, I'm not asking for something from you that you're not willing to give. I promise.'

And he knew he'd driven her to that confession. Knew she thought he'd had cold feet and, hell, he *had*. Except now he felt his heart twist and turn inside him and he wanted her all over again, in his bed, in his life.

'Come here,' he murmured, and kissed her, slow and deep. She kissed him back, her hands fisting in his hair, her body pressed hard against his.

Somehow they made it to the bed, stumbling and tripping, shedding clothes. She pulled him down on top of her, hands sliding over skin, drawing him closer. 'I want to touch you,' she muttered against his throat, licking the salt from his skin. 'Last time I never got to touch you.'

And he wanted to be touched. He rolled over on his back, let out a shuddering sigh as he spread his arms wide, submitted to her desires. 'Touch me, Scary. Touch me all you want.'

She laughed and slowly ran her hand down his chest, across the smooth skin of his hip, and then wrapped her hand around his erection. 'All I want?'

'Hell, yes.'

She laughed again low in her throat, a seductress filled with power. He liked—no, he *loved*—seeing her this way, confident, strong, sensual. She kissed her way down his chest, lingering in certain places, blitzing quick caresses in others, and left his whole body on fire. His hands tangled in her hair as she moved lower.

'Millie…'

'You said all I want,' she reminded him huskily, and took him in her mouth.

Lord have mercy. He closed his eyes, all thought obliterating as she moved on him. All he could feel was Millie. All he could think was Millie.

Millie.

His hips jerked and he let out a cry; she moved so quickly he barely registered the change as she sank on top of him so he filled her up and she set the pace, her hands behind her, braced on his thighs. Chase didn't have much left in him. He grabbed hold of her hips and arched to meet her, his eyes closed, his head thrown back, everything in him a surrender.

A joy.

'Millie,' he said aloud, groaning her name. 'Millie.'

She came on top of him, her body tensing gloriously and then drooping over him as her hair brushed his cheek and she let out a long, well-satisfied sigh.

Chase let out another shuddering breath. This woman was going to kill him if she kept this up. He felt the thunder of his heart, and knew it was more of a danger than he ever really wanted to admit.

But it would be a wonderful way to die.

CHAPTER NINE

MILLIE gazed out at the ocean, little more than a *shooshing* of waves in the darkness. A tiny sliver of moonlight glinted off the dark waters. The air felt cool now, chilling her overheated skin. Chase had fallen asleep after they'd made love—no, *had sex*—and she'd dozed for a bit before, restless, she'd prowled out here and come to sit on the hard, cool sand by the shore, her knees drawn up to her chest.

The problem, she thought, was for her it *had* been making love. Love, that dreaded word, that fearful concept. She was falling in love with him and had a terrible feeling it was too late to stop the descent. And descent is what it was, straight down to hell, to that underworld of fear and guilt where every day you wondered if this would be your last one of happiness.

Plenty of people, she reminded herself, had second chances. Plenty of people were bereaved and moved on with life, found someone else to risk it all for. Plenty of people, but not her. She just didn't think she was made that way, couldn't imagine breaking her heart all over again.

And what about Chase? Even if he was interested in taking their fling past this week, he'd surely want more than she could give. Marriage, maybe even children. The thought had a shudder of both longing and terror ripping through her.

All foolish fairy-tales, anyway, because Chase wasn't interested in any of that. He'd wanted the fun back, just like she had wanted, but no more. And she got that now. They'd play by his rules from now on, and they would be her rules too.

'I wondered where you'd gone.'

Millie stiffened at the sound of Chase's sleep-husked voice. He made her think of rumpled bed covers and salty skin. The way she'd abandoned herself to him just a few hours ago and how she'd gloried in it.

'I couldn't sleep.'

She heard the whisper of sand as he came closer. 'No?'

'No. I'm afraid I'm a bit of an insomniac. Comes with the job, unfortunately.'

'Have you checked the stock market today?' Chase asked, only half-teasing, but Millie stiffened in sudden realisation.

She hadn't. She hadn't checked the stock market in over forty-eight hours. Good Lord.

'Of course,' she answered breezily, but it was a beat too late.

'Liar,' Chase said softly, and came to sit beside her, clad only in boxers, his bare thigh inches from her own. She'd been intimate with him in so many ways, yet the feel of his leg next to hers still gave her the shivers.

'If I haven't checked, it's only because I can't get reception on your boat.'

'You're a terrible liar, you know that? You haven't checked because you haven't thought of it, and that scares you more than anything.'

Millie said nothing. She was falling in love with him, and even though her body still tingled from where it had been joined to his she knew it was the last thing he wanted.

'The stock market will live without me for a few days.'

'I suppose the more relevant question is, will you live without it?'

She angled her head so she was half-facing him, but she

couldn't make out his expression in the darkness. 'I'm here, aren't I?'

'Why did you leave my bed?'

'Oh, is this some caveman thing? Or is it just playboy pride?'

'Playboy pride?'

'You know, you've got to be the one who walks away first.' She tried to keep her voice light and teasing—banter, damn it—but she knew she'd failed. Chase didn't answer, and when he finally spoke it was too soft, too sad.

'I'm not walking away, Millie.'

'Yet. You have four more days, remember, and I take contract violations very seriously.'

Chase didn't say anything and Millie felt herself start to go brittle. Keeping up her side of the bargain was exacting a high price. Why couldn't he play along? Wasn't that what he wanted?

'When did things start to go wrong with your husband?' *What?* Millie froze, stared straight ahead. 'Is that why you still feel guilty?'

She drew a strangled breath. 'Why are you asking me these things now?'

'Because I should have asked them before. When you wanted to tell me.'

'Should have,' she repeated, and Chase gave a little nod. 'I know.'

She shook her head, decisive now. Needing to be. 'Look, Chase, I fully admit I was kind of vulnerable after we—after we had sex.' It had been so much than just sex. So much more than what she'd thought she wanted. 'That was kind of the whole point of the exercise, wasn't it?' she added, still trying, desperately, to tease.

'Are you calling the best sex you've ever an *exercise*?'

The best sex she'd ever had. And she couldn't deny it,

because it was true. Even if it hadn't been just sex. 'You know what I mean.'

'I know I wanted you to lose control but then I didn't know what to do when you did. I'm sorry for that.'

'Yeah. Well.' She scooped up a handful of damp sand and let it trickle through her fingers. 'It doesn't really matter.'

'How can you say that?'

'Because it's true. That—that conversation was just a momentary weakness. I'm over it now.'

'I'm not.'

She felt the first prickle of annoyance. 'Why are you doing this? I thought you'd be relieved.'

'You were going to tell me something else, something more than what you'd already told me.'

'No, I wasn't.'

'The real reason you carry all this sadness around. The reason you can't let it go.'

She felt her heart freeze in her chest, so for a moment she couldn't breathe. Couldn't think. 'If I seem sad, it's because my husband and—because my husband died. I think that would be obvious.' She turned to glare at him, forced herself to keep that angry stare.

Chase looked levelly back, eyes slightly narrowed, thinking. Figuring her out. 'If you won't tell me,' he said quietly, 'then maybe I should guess.'

'*Guess*?'

'Just like I did with your apartment and job and whole lifestyle.'

'Don't.'

'I know I messed up, Millie, but I want to make it right now.'

'It's too late.' She hugged her knees to her chest, amazed that even in the Caribbean she felt cold. *Icy*. 'Why bother anyway, Chase? We only have a few more days together.'

He had no answer to that, and she didn't expect him to. He still only wanted a week.

Chase stared at Millie's taut profile and tried to order his thoughts. He had to get this right. For an instant he'd wondered if he should stop pushing her, but a deeper instinct told him she needed this. Regardless of what did or didn't happen between them, she needed this reckoning. This release.

The only trouble was, he had no idea what sorrow she was still hiding.

'So.' He let out a long, considering breath. 'You said you and your husband grew apart over different things.' No answer. He really didn't have a clue how to go about this. Mentally he reviewed the facts he knew about Millie Lang: she was a hedge-fund manager; she'd been married; her semi-estranged husband had died in a car accident two years ago. Those were the basics, but what else?

She bit her lip when she was anxious. She was obsessive about work. She'd mentioned someone named Charlotte…

Charlotte.

Her words just now came back to him, and gears clicked into place. *If I seem sad, it's because my husband and— because my husband died.*

Someone else had died in that accident. Someone, he suspected, named Charlotte.

'Was your husband having an affair?' he asked quietly and she stared at him in blatant surprise.

'Why on earth would you think that?'

'You said you grew apart.' He racked his brain. 'Over different things.'

'Not that far apart.'

'So what did you disagree on?'

'It doesn't matter.'

'That is so far from the truth, Millie, that it's almost funny.' He laid one hand on her wrist, felt the desperate flutter of her pulse under his fingers. 'It matters so much you made me promise not to talk about your past at all.'

'I *told* you about my past.'

'Not all of it.' Of that he was certain.

'Enough,' she whispered, and it was a confession. There was more. There was more she wasn't telling him and, while he might not need to know, she needed to tell. He knew that, knew it with the same instinctive certainty that he'd known how to make her come alive in his arms.

He decided to risk a shot in the dark. 'Why do you never talk about Charlotte?'

Her mouth gaped open silently; he would have found her expression funny in almost any other situation. Now he found it heartbreaking. She looked like he'd just punched her in the gut. Like he'd broken her heart.

'Don't,' she finally whispered, and there was so much pain in her voice he almost backed down. He almost took her in his arms and told her he wouldn't ask anything more if she'd just smile and tease him again.

'Charlotte died in the accident with your husband,' he said instead, and heard how raw his own voice sounded. This was hard for him too. 'Didn't she?'

Millie just gave a little shake of her head, her gaze unfocused, and Chase knew she was still asking him to stop. He wouldn't.

'Who was she, Millie? Someone important to you, obviously.' She said nothing, just set her jaw and stared out to sea. Chase's first thought was that Charlotte had been her husband's mistress. Someone Millie refused to talk about or acknowledge. But as he gazed at her set profile he realised that was totally off. He knew Millie better than that. Charlotte wasn't somebody she'd hated; she was somebody she'd *loved*. Millie didn't talk about emotion or affection, and certainly not love. And, if she was willing to talk about her husband's death but not Charlotte's, then this Charlotte had to be someone even more precious to her.

Then it came to him. And it was so obvious and awful that for a moment he couldn't speak. He pictured Millie only hours ago, naked above him, and remembered those two silvery lines that had wavered just under her navel. He was a guy, and he didn't know a lot about that kind of stuff, but he still knew what they were.

Stretch marks.

'Charlotte was your daughter, wasn't she?' he said quietly, and in answer Millie let out a soft cry and buried her face in her hands.

Chase felt his heart pound and his own throat tighten with emotion. 'She died in the accident with your husband.' Millie's shoulders shook and Chase felt his eyes sting. 'Oh, Millie. I'm sorry. I'm so sorry.' Then he pulled her into his arms, just the comfort of his embrace, because he didn't have any words. She didn't resist, just buried her face in the curve of his neck as her body shook with the force of her sobs.

He thought she'd cried before, when they'd made love. He thought he'd breached all of her defences then, but he knew now she'd clung to this last desperate barrier. Her sobs were torn from deep within her, the raw, guttural sounds of an animal in pain.

Chase stroked her back, her hair, murmured words he wasn't even aware he was saying. 'Sweetheart, it's OK to cry. Let yourself cry, Millie. Let yourself cry, my love.'

My love. Distantly the words penetrated the haze of his own feeling. He loved her. Of course he did. It didn't even surprise him. It felt too right for that.

Chase didn't know how long Millie cried, how long he sat there holding her in his arms, the night soft and dark all around them. Time ceased to matter.

Eventually, after minutes or hours, Millie pulled away from him and sniffed.

'Rob wanted me to get an abortion. That's when things started to go wrong.' Chase didn't speak, just gazed at her steadily, his hand folded over hers. He wasn't going through the motions this time. He was feeling it, all of it, and it *hurt*. Loving someone—feeling her pain—it hurt.

Millie let out a shuddering breath. 'We'd been dating since college, but we waited to get married. We wanted everything to be right—our careers established, to be able to buy our own apartment. We'd thought about kids, but decided not to try till later. Rob was a lawyer, and he was completely focused on his career, like I was on mine. We both liked it that way.' She stared at him almost fiercely, as if he had disagreed. 'We *did*.'

'I believe you,' he said quietly.

'Then I fell pregnant, several years before we planned on starting a family. I was thirty.' She fell silent, lost in memory, and Chase just stroked his fingers over hers, light little touches to remind her that he was here. He was listening. 'I was surprised,' she said slowly, 'but I was OK with it. It was a few years earlier than we'd planned, but…' She shrugged. 'I thought we'd adjust.'

'And your husband didn't?'

'Rob wanted to become partner before we had kids. It was really important to him, and I understood that. We'd had a plan, and he wanted to stick to it.' She glanced at him with wide, troubled eyes. 'Don't hate him.'

Don't hate him? Of course he hated him. He hated everything about the selfish bastard. Chase squeezed her hand. 'I think it's more important that you don't hate him.'

'I don't,' she said quickly. 'I never did. I felt…sad. And guilty, like it was my fault for changing the plan.'

'It takes two, you know.'

She gave a tiny, mirthless smile. 'I know. But it was creating a lot of stress in our marriage, and so… I agreed to have the abortion.'

Chase's fingers stilled on hers. This he hadn't expected. 'You did?'

She nodded, biting her lip hard as a single tear tracked its way down her cheek. 'I did. I'd convinced myself it was for the best. That our marriage was more important than—than a baby.' She glanced down at her lap, wiping away that one tear with her fingers. 'I couldn't go through it. I went to the appointment, and I sat in the waiting room, and when they called my name…I was literally sick.'

'You have a habit of doing that in tense situations.'

She let out a soft huff of shaky laughter. 'Emotional situations. When it comes to buying and selling stock I have nerves of steel.'

'I bet.'

'I went home and told Rob I couldn't do it. And he accepted that. He did.' She glanced up quickly. 'I'm not revising history, I promise. He wasn't a bad man. I loved him.'

Chase said nothing. He didn't trust himself to offer an opinion on Rob. 'And then she was born,' Millie said softly. 'And she was beautiful. I never thought I was particularly maternal, and in a lot of ways I wasn't. I never got the hang of breastfeeding, and I couldn't even fold up the stroller.' She gave a little shake of her head. 'That thing always defeated me.'

'There are more important things.'

'I know. And I loved her. I did.' She sounded like she was trying to convince him, and Chase had no idea why. He'd never doubt Millie's love for her child. She might hate talking about emotions, but she had them. She could love someone deeply—if she let herself. And if the person she loved let her.

'I went back to work when Charlotte was three weeks old,'

Millie said after a moment. She sounded subdued now, her voice flattening out. 'I had to. Hedge-fund managers don't get a lot of maternity leave. It's still a man's field. And I worked long hours—ten- and twelve-hour days. We had a nanny, Lucinda. She saw a hell of a lot more of Charlotte than I did.'

'That doesn't make you a bad mother.'

'No.' Millie was silent for a moment, her eyes reddened and puffy, her face set in its familiar determined lines. 'But if someone had told me that I would only have her for two years, if I had ever realised how short my time with her would be...' She paused, looking up at Chase with such bleakness that he fought not to cry himself. 'I would have quit my job in an instant. In a *heartbeat*.'

'No one ever knows that kind of thing,' he said quietly. His throat was so clogged his voice came out hoarse. 'No one can ever know how long they have.' He certainly didn't.

'I know. But I wish I had thought of it. I wish I had realised. I wish—' Her voice broke, and she forced herself to continue. 'I wish I had said goodbye when Rob took her out that day. They were going to a petting farm out on Long Island. And I had to go into the office—on a Saturday—and was in a tizz about some client's meltdown. So I pushed them both out the door and didn't look back once.'

'Oh, Millie.' He took her in his arms again, this time because he needed to touch her. He pressed his cheek against the warm silk of her hair and closed his eyes, then repeated his question. 'Why don't you ever talk about Charlotte?'

'I can't. Couldn't.' Her voice was muffled against his chest. 'My family understood, they waited for me to talk first, and I never did. People at work felt too awkward, so they said nothing. I went to all the counselling and support groups and just talked about Rob. I could talk about that, I could say all the right things. But Charlotte...' Her voice choked. 'God, I miss her so much.' And then she began to cry again, silent, shaking sobs. 'I want to move on, I want to be happy again, but I'm terrified,' she said through her tears. 'Terrified of forgetting her somehow, and terrified to lose someone again.' She dragged her arm across her eyes. 'I could never go through that heartache again.'

Chase felt as if her words were falling into the emptiness inside him, echoing through all that silence. *I could never.* 'Of course you couldn't,' he murmured, and as he continued to stroke her hair, her back, holding her so achingly close, he felt the hope that had been blooming inside him wither and die.

Millie stared at the sand, wiping her cheeks of the last of her tears. Her body felt weak and boneless with exhaustion. She'd never cried so much, not even when she'd first learned of her husband and daughter's deaths. Yet they had been good tears this time. Healing tears. Telling Chase about Charlotte had been like lancing a wound. Painful and necessary, and now afterwards, she felt a surprising and thankful relief.

She glanced up at him, felt a rush of love at his serious expression, his eyes shadowed with concern. She loved him. She loved him for making her laugh, but she loved him more for making her cry. He'd known she needed to. He knew her so well, had known her since he'd first crossed the beach to ask her why she wasn't painting.

'Thank you,' she said softly, and Chase gave a small smile and nodded. She reached over and laced her fingers with his. He squeezed her hand and that reassured her. She wasn't exactly sure what he was thinking, or if he was freaked out now, the way he had been when she'd first told him about Rob. She didn't know what the future could possibly hold.

After all this, did Chase still want to walk away in another few days? Did she?

Loving someone was painful, messy, hard. And wonderful. Life-sustaining. Now that she'd felt all that again, could she even think of living without it?

'Let's go back to bed,' Chase said, and tugged her gently to her feet. Millie followed him back into the hut, slid into bed and pulled the cool linen sheets over both their bodies.

For a single second they both lay there, not touching, and her heart felt suspended in her chest. Then Chase pulled her to him, tucking her body to curve around his, his arm around her waist, his fingers threaded with hers.

Millie felt all the tension, anxiety and sadness leave her body in a fast, flowing river, and all that was left was tiredness—and peace. She closed her eyes, her lips curving in a tiny smile of true contentment, and slept.

When she woke she was alone in bed, and sunlight filtered through the net curtains that blew in the ocean breeze. Millie rolled over in bed, blinked up at the grass roof as memories and emotions tumbled through her. Then she smiled.

She slipped on her discarded silk shift, because even though the cove they were in was private she didn't know how private. Then she stepped out of the hut onto the sun-warmed sand and went in search of Chase.

There weren't many places for him to go, unless he'd gone over to the main part of the resort to fetch them some breakfast. He wasn't on their little stretch of beach, or anywhere in sight. Deciding he must have gone for breakfast after all, she went to the separate enclosure that housed the bathroom facilities, including a sumptuous, sunken tub of blue-black granite. She'd just stepped into the little hut, a smile still on her face, when she stilled. Tried to process the sight in front of her.

Chase lay on the floor, his face the colour of chalk, unconscious.

CHAPTER TEN

MILLIE didn't know how long she stood there staring, her mind seeming to have frozen in shocked disbelief. Too long, but finally she moved forward, knelt down, and tried to feel his pulse with fingers too numb to feel anything.

Finally she was able to detect his pulse, but she had no idea if it was normal. It seemed thin and thready, but maybe all pulses did.

'Chase.' She touched his face; his skin felt clammy. Her stomach cramped. '*Chase.*'

Nothing.

What had happened? What was *wrong* with him?

Taking a shuddering breath, Millie rose from the cold stone floor of the hut and hurried back to their sleeping accommodation. She scrabbled through her handbag for her mobile phone, the phone she hadn't checked in days.

'Please…' she whispered, and breathed a silent prayer of relief when she saw the row of bars that indicated reception. Then she dialled 911. She realised she didn't even know if Anguilla had emergency services, or a 911 number, so when she heard someone answer she nearly wept.

The questions the operator fired at her made her brain freeze again.

'Where are you located?'

'A resort...' She scrambled to remember the name. 'Cap something.'

'Cap Juluca?'

'Yes.'

'Can you tell me what happened?'

'I don't know. I went into the bathroom and he was just lying there, unconscious. I—I can't wake him up.' Terror temporarily closed her throat as memories attacked her.

There's been an accident. Critical condition... Come immediately...

When she'd got to the hospital, it had been too late.

Now, as if from a great distance, she heard the woman on the other end of the line tell her an ambulance would be coming within ten minutes.

'Please go to the scene of the accident and wait.'

The scene of the accident. The words caused an instinctive, visceral response to rise up in her and she almost gagged. She could not believe this was happening again.

The stone was cold under her bare knees as she knelt by Chase, held his cold hand and waited for the ambulance to come. Once he stirred, eyelids fluttering, and hope rose like a wild thing inside her, beating with hard, desperate wings. Then he lapsed back into unconsciousness and she bit her lip so hard she tasted blood. In the distance she heard the mournful, urgent wail of the ambulance.

The next hour passed in a blur of shock and fear. Still unconscious, Chase was loaded into the ambulance. Millie went with him, tried to answer questions she had no idea about.

Does he have any medical conditions you know about?

Does he take any medications?

Does he have any allergies?

She couldn't answer a single one. She felt swamped with ignorance, drowning in it. She loved him, she loved him so much, yet in this moment she couldn't help him. She could do nothing…just as before.

At one point in that endless ride to the hospital Chase regained consciousness, his eyelids fluttering before he opened his eyes and focused blearily on her. Millie's heart leapt into her throat.

'Chase…'

He smiled and relief flooded through her. It was all going to be OK. Everything, him, *them*, was going to be all right. Then he glanced around and she saw comprehension come coldly to him. That joyous light winked out and he turned his head away from her. Millie put her hand over his; Chase moved his away. She swallowed, trying not to feel the sting of rejection. They were in an ambulance; everything was confused, nerve-wracking. It didn't mean anything.

She ended up sitting in the emergency waiting room, exhausted and chilled despite the sultry Caribbean air, waiting for someone to tell her something. Anything.

Finally a nurse came through the double door and clicked her way across the tile floor. 'Mr Bryant may see you now,' she said, and with murmured thanks Millie followed her back through those double doors and into a utilitarian hospital room. Chase was sitting up in the bed, his face pale but otherwise looking healthy. Looking like himself. Relief poured through her just at the sight of him, healthy, whole, safe.

'Chase.' She started forward, wanting to cling to him but hanging back because she still didn't know what had happened.

'Hello, Millie.'

'Did they find out what happened to you? I saw you on the bathroom floor and I was so scared—but you're all right?' She glanced at him as if checking for signs of—what? Chase wasn't saying anything. He wasn't even looking at her. 'Chase?' she asked uncertainly, her voice seeming to echo through the room, and finally he looked at her.

'I have leukaemia, Millie.'

'Wh-what?' The words felt like no more than a jumble of syllables, nonsensical. 'Did they just *tell* you that? Because surely they'd have to do all sorts of tests first?'

He shook his head, the movement one of impatience. 'I've known for eight months and…' He let out a weary breath. 'Nine days. I passed out this morning because I'm on a new medication that can cause dizziness. I had a dizzy spell and hit my head on the tub.'

Millie just blinked. Her mind was spinning in hopeless circles, still unable to make sense of what he'd said. 'You have leukaemia?' she finally asked, as if he hadn't just told her.

'Chronic myeloid leukaemia.'

She sank slowly into a chair, simply because her legs would no longer hold her. She stared at him, speechless, while he gazed back all too evenly. She could not tell what he was feeling, but she was pretty sure it wasn't good.

'I'm sorry,' she finally said, and he inclined his head in cool acknowledgement. 'Why…?' Her throat was so dry she had to wait a moment to swallow and be able to speak. 'Why didn't you tell me?'

'You can really ask me that?'

'You didn't want me to know?'

'Obviously.'

She recoiled a bit, hurt by the coolness in his tone. Why was he pushing her away *now*? 'I can understand that, Chase, but I thought— I thought after I'd—' She stopped, unwilling to articulate what she'd hoped and believed when he was gazing at her so evenly, so *unhelpfully*. 'Tell me more,' she finally whispered.

'More?'

'About the leukaemia.'

He shrugged. 'What do you want to know? It's leukae-mia, Millie. Bone cancer. I take a medication which keeps it under control but my symptoms had started getting worse, so my doctor switched to a different inhibitor. That's why I was on St Julian's—to see how the medication affected me before I returned to New York.'

'You should have told me,' she said quietly, knowing it was the wrong thing to say—or at least the wrong time to say it. Yet she couldn't help herself. She'd bared herself to him, body and soul, and he'd kept all his secrets and emotions tucked firmly away.

'There was no reason to tell you.'

'No *reason*? What kind of relationship can we have if—?'

'We don't have a relationship, Millie.'

Millie stared, her mouth still open, her heart starting to thud. She didn't like the way Chase was looking at her, with steely certainty. Gone was any remnant of the laughing, light-hearted man she'd come to love. 'Chase,' she said, her voice so low it reverberated in her chest. She felt the awful sting of tears.

'We've had our intense week.'

'Actually,' she managed, and now her throat ached with the effort of holding all that emotion back, 'we have three more days.'

'They're keeping me in hospital overnight, so we'll have to cut it short.'

'You're *reneging*?' she asked, trying desperately to manage some levity, and for a second she thought she'd reached him, saw a lightening in his eyes and prayed silently for him to stop this. To see what they had and know that it was *good*.

'Consider our contract terminated,' he said flatly and looked away.

Millie stared at him and clenched her fists in helpless

anger. She couldn't fight this. And why should she? Chase was keeping to their original terms. She was the one who had changed, who now wanted more. So much more.

'How am I supposed to get back to St Julian's?'

He hesitated, and she knew he was debating whether to tell her to charter a boat by herself. Then with a shrug he said, 'I'll take you back tomorrow, if you want to stay at Cap Juluca another night.'

'All right. Thank you.' She'd take it, because she wasn't ready to walk away for good. She needed time to think, to figure out her next move.

'It won't change anything, Millie,' he said, the words a bleak warning, and she gazed at him coolly.

'Everything's already changed, Chase. But I think you know that.'

In a numb fog of swirling despair she took a taxi back to the resort and arranged to stay another night. She paused on the threshold of the grass hut where they'd spent last night as lovers. Her heart wrung like a rag at the sight of that low, wide bed, the linen sheets now pulled tightly across, the scattered clothes now folded neatly on a wooden chest. She sank onto the bed, then sank her face into her hands. She felt so much sorrow, yet she couldn't cry. She had no more tears left; she'd given them all to Chase. They'd been tears for her pain, yet now she felt a grief for his.

Leukaemia.

He'd known for eight months. And he'd been keeping it to himself, of that Millie had no doubt. She wondered if even his brothers knew. She imagined Chase keeping up that light, laughing front even as he battled with his diagnosis. Had his lightness been his refuge, his way of coping? Or had it been his armour, the only way to keep prying people and their awful pity at bay?

She knew how it went. She understood how it felt to be defined by pain, and she even understood why Chase hadn't told her.

Yet it was different now. *They* were different, because she'd broken down her own barriers with Chase's help, and now she needed to help him break down his own.

How?

Millie left the hut for the smooth expanse of sand. From their private cove she couldn't see another building or person, just a few sailboats bobbing on the aquamarine waves. It was a gorgeous afternoon, a cloudless blue sky and a bright lemon sun. The sand sparkled under its rays. She wished Chase were here, wanted to see him with his feet planted in the sand and his face tilted up to that healing sun. She didn't like to picture him in a hospital room in a paper gown, living with the reality of his disease.

Even now she fought that reality. How could he be sick, when he looked so healthy? When he brimmed with vitality and life? Yet even as she asked herself these pointless questions another part of her mind remembered how he'd winced when she'd landed on him from the boat; how he'd squinted into the sunset with a grim focus. How he'd told her he wanted to seize life, suck the marrow from its bones.

Now she understood why. He didn't know how long he had to do it.

Part of her shrank in terror from that thought. Part of her wanted to run away, to forget. She didn't need the pain of losing someone again. She didn't know if she could survive it.

And yet. She had to fight for it, because life simply wasn't worth living without him. Without the love he'd given and shown her. The love she felt straight through to her soul.

Millie took a deep, cleansing breath. So she'd fight. And

that meant fighting Chase. Which meant she needed to throw down her armour…and find some weapons.

Chase stared at the doctor who had come in to give him the news. What news, he didn't yet know, but he knew enough not to expect anything good. Living with chronic leukaemia was a slow descent into disability. Into death.

'Your blood work has come back,' she said, closing the door behind her. Chase braced himself. He had his bloods done routinely and he knew what numbers he needed to stay in the chronic phase. If—when—he moved up to the accelerated phase, his days starting looking very numbered.

'And?' he asked tersely, because she was still scanning the lab report and not actually giving him information.

'They look fairly good.'

What did that mean? 'Fairly good' wasn't great. It wasn't fabulous or terrific or any of the other words he would have preferred. 'Fairly?' he repeated.

'Your platelet count is around two-hundred thousand. Which, as you probably know, is stable.'

Not that stable. It had been higher two weeks ago, when he'd first switched to the new inhibitor. It was clearly dropping, and that was not good at all.

'When you return to New York you should get your blood work done again,' the doctor said, and Chase just kept himself from saying, *Well, duh.* 'And reassess the effectiveness of your prescription.'

Again, obvious. Chase leaned his head against the pillow and felt the dread he'd banished for nearly a week creep back. The dread he hadn't felt since he'd met Millie, and fallen in love with her prickly self.

He quickly banished the thought, steeled himself to live without the exact thing that had been bringing him joy. *Millie.* There was no way, absolutely no way at all, he could burden her with this. *I could never go through that heart-ache again.* She'd spoken in a moment of raw grief and re-membrance, but Chase knew she'd meant it with every fibre of her being. She might think she felt differently right now, but he knew she didn't really want this. Him. If she shackled herself to him, there was every chance she would go through that same heartache—and who even knew how soon.

He spent a restless night in the hospital; he'd always hated the sterile rooms, the antiseptic smell, the sense of sorrow that permeated the very air like some invisible, noxious gas. His thoughts kept him awake too, for his irritating brain—or maybe it was his even more contrary heart—kept remem-bering and reliving every second he'd spent with Millie over the last four days.

Four days. He'd known her for four damned days. There was no way he should be as cut up about losing her as he was. He barely knew her. A week ago—one single week—he hadn't even known she'd existed.

And yet, a life without her seemed like a sepia-toned pho-tograph, leached of colour and even life. He couldn't imagine it, even as he grimly acknowledged that that was just what he'd be doing this time tomorrow.

Morning came, storm clouds a violet smudge on the hori-zon. A storm was going to kick up, the nurse told him, which meant rough sailing from here to St Julian's. He debated calling it off, telling Millie he couldn't sail in this weather, but he wasn't about to back down now. Besides, if he knew Millie—which he knew he did—she wasn't going to give up without a fight. He'd seen how shocked she'd looked when he'd ended it yesterday, had known she'd been think-ing they'd have something after this week. And how could she not, after all they'd shared? She'd cried in his arms. He'd held her heart. And now he was breaking it, which made him a stupid, heartless jerk because he should have known from the first that this was a likely outcome.

He'd known he was a lousy deal, and yet he'd convinced himself that one week would work. Would be enough for a woman like Millie—or a man like him. And they could both walk away with their heart and souls intact.

Ha.

As he left the hospital, the sky still cloudless blue despite the gathering storm clouds on the horizon, Chase had a sudden, fierce hope that he could turn this around. The statistics for the long-term survival rate of CML were good. *Excellent*, his doctor had assured him as she'd handed him rafts of literature. Chase had hated even the titles: *Coping with CML; Accepting Your Diagnosis.* Talk about a buzz-kill. It had all felt incredibly negative, while putting a desperately positive spin on something that just sucked. Basically, what happened with CML or any disease? You degenerated and then you died. End of story.

And so this was the end of his and Millie's story, brief chapter that it had been.

I could never go through that heartache again.

Well, Chase thought, she wouldn't. He'd make sure of it.

He kept up all of his steely resolve until he actually saw Millie. She was waiting for him in the grass hut where they'd made love and just seeing her there reminded him of how she'd lain on top of him, how she'd taken him into herself. How he'd felt so good. So loved.

Now she sat on the edge of the bed, her face pale and set, her silk shift-dress hopelessly wrinkled which, considering the usual state of her clothes, had to be driving her crazy.

Except she didn't seem aware of it at all.

She stared at him with eyes the colour of her dress, brown, warm and soft, just like she was. How had he ever thought she was hard or severe? Scary, he'd called her, and it had turned into an endearment, but it just seemed silly now. She was softness, warmth and light. She was love.

'You've been biting your lip again.'

She touched the deep red marks in the lush softness of her mouth. 'Old habits die hard, I guess.'

Chase thought about making some quip back, but then decided he didn't want to do the banter. It wasn't going anywhere; they weren't. Except back to St Julian's, and on to New York. The rest of their lives apart.

'You ready to go?'

'Fortunately I didn't bring much.'

He didn't say anything, just took one look at the handbag she'd left at her feet. It was one of those bulky hold-all types and he reached for it. She flung out one fluttering hand.

'I can get it.'

Chase stiffened. 'I can manage a single bag, Millie. Despite how you saw me earlier, I'm perfectly—' Healthy? No. 'Fine.' For the moment.

'I know you are,' she said quietly. 'I wasn't saying that, Chase.'

'Let's go.'

She stared at him for a second, her eyes still so dark and soft, and just one look had Chase's steely resolve start to rust and crumble. He wanted to take her in his arms. No, he wanted her to take *him* in her arms. He wanted to cry in her arms like she had in his.

The thought appalled him.

'Coming?' he demanded tersely, and with a single nod she rose from the bed.

They didn't speak as they walked through the lush gardens of the resort, or in the cab the concierge called for them that took them back to where his boat was moored in Meads Bay. No words even as he helped her into the boat and set sail.

No, Millie waited until they were out on open water running towards St Julian's to begin her attack. And that was what it felt like, the same as when she'd begun her battle to sleep with him. Now she battled to stay.

'Did they do blood work in the hospital?'

'Some.'

'What were the results?'

Chase shaded his eyes against the sun, gazed at the thickening clouds boiling on the horizon, spreading out. Damn. The storm was moving faster than he'd anticipated. He was a confident sailor, but after a sleepless night spent in hospital, not to mention his reaction to his new meds, he wasn't thrilled about riding out a storm. Especially not with Millie.

'Chase?' she prompted softly and he sighed.

'I don't really want to talk about this, Millie.'

'Why not?'

'Because there's no point. We had our week and now we're finished.' He took a breath, made himself be harsh. 'You don't have any part of my life any more.'

'I'm not sure I had any part of your life.'

He didn't say anything, didn't even shrug. She was probably right, even if it hadn't felt that way to him. It felt like she'd had a huge part of his life, a huge part of his *self*, but he wasn't about to hand her that ammunition.

'Chase, I think you care for me.'

Again no response. Silence was easier. He kept staring out at the horizon, until he felt a hard shove in his shoulder. He turned, astonished, to see Millie glaring at him.

'*Don't* give me the silent treatment. That is so cowardly.'

He felt a bolt of sudden rage. 'Are you calling me a coward?'

'If the shoe fits.'

He opened his mouth to issue some scathing retort, but

none came. She was right. He *was* being a coward. 'I'm sorry,' he finally said. 'You're right.'

'Wait, you're actually agreeing with me?'

He sighed, not wanting to joke with her even as he craved it. Craved her. 'Millie…'

'Don't do this, Chase. Don't throw away what we have.'

'We don't have anything.'

'Now you're a coward *and* a liar.'

'Call me what you want.'

'Look me in the eye and tell me you don't care for me,' Millie ordered.

Obliging her would be the easiest way out of this. 'Millie, I don't care for you.'

'In the eye, I said.'

He'd been staring at her chin. Reluctantly he raised his gaze to those dark, soft eyes—and felt himself sink into their warmth. Damn it. He couldn't say it. He knew he couldn't. He swallowed. Stared. Said nothing.

Millie smiled. 'See? You do.'

Fine, he'd be honest. 'You're right, I do. It was an intense few days, and naturally that created feelings in both of us.'

'So now you're trying the "it's not real" route.'

'How can we know it's real?' Chase argued. 'We've been on an island paradise, Millie. We haven't seen each other in action, in our homes and jobs and lives. How do we even know this will stand the test of a stressful week, much less time?'

She bit her lip. 'Well, there's only one way to find that out.'

He'd walked right into that one. 'I don't want to.'

'What are you afraid of?'

Dying. Dying alone. 'Millie, you said yourself you didn't want to go through that heartache again. You couldn't.'

Her eyes widened, lips parting. 'Is that what this is about? You're protecting me?'

'I have a terminal disease, Millie. Death is, at some point, a certainty.'

'Guess what, Chase? I have a terminal disease too. It's called life, and death is also a certainty for me.'

He almost smiled at that one, but he shook his head instead. 'Don't be flippant. I'm serious.'

'So am I.' She took a breath, launched into her second line of attack. 'I did the research.'

'What, on your phone?'

'As a matter of fact, yes. The long-term survival rate for CML patients is eighty-seven percent.'

He'd read the same statistic, probably on the same encyclopaedia website. 'For those who have it detected early enough.'

'Did you?'

'Maybe.' The doctor had given him a good prognosis, but then his platelets had fallen and the first inhibitor had stopped working. He could be staring at an accelerated phase within the year, or even sooner. He could be in that other thirteen percent.

'And after five years of living with CML,' Millie continued steadily, 'the rate rises to ninety-three percent, which is the same kind of life expectancy as a person without CML. Stuff happens, Chase. Accidents, diseases, life. There are no guarantees.' Her voice wavered slightly. 'Trust me, I know that.'

'I know you do. Which is why I don't want you to go through it again.' He decided he needed to be brutal, even if it hurt both of them. 'Millie, if we were married, if we'd known each other and been in love with each other for years, then yes, I'd expect you there by my side. I'd want you there. But we've known each other five days. Five *days*. And, yes, they were intense—and I'll admit it, they were some of the best days of my life. But that's all they were. Days. And with that little history you don't shackle yourself to someone who is a losing proposition.'

She blinked. Bit her lip. 'Shouldn't I be the one to decide that?'

He sighed wearily. She was the strongest, most stubborn woman he'd ever met, and even though he admired her tenacity he couldn't cope with it any more. 'We can't talk about this any more.'

'We *can't*?'

'No.' Grimly he pointed to the sky. It had been a sweet, clear blue half an hour ago, but now those violet clouds had boiled right up over the boat. The brisk breeze that had them on a good run back to St Julian's was picking up into a dangerous wind. 'A storm's coming,' he said. 'We need to secure the boat and you need to get below.'

CHAPTER ELEVEN

MILLIE stared at the thunderous clouds overhead and felt her stomach freefall. This didn't look good. The intensity of their conversation evaporated in light of a far more intense reality.

'What do you want me to do?' she asked, and Chase didn't even look at her as he responded.

'Get down below.'

'But you'll need help up here.'

'Millie, you aren't an experienced sailor. Having you up here is more of a liability than a help.' He glanced at her and she saw real fear in his eyes. 'Get down below.'

Millie hesitated. 'I don't want you to be up here alone.'

'I assure you,' he said coldly, 'I am perfectly competent.'

'You know, always assuming I am making some reference to CML is really annoying,' she flashed back. 'I wouldn't want anyone up here alone, Chase. It's dangerous. And I can be very good at obeying instructions.'

His mouth *almost* quirked. Or so Millie hoped. 'You could have fooled me.'

'Tell me what to do.'

'I'm sure that's the last time I'll hear *that* phrase from your lips. All right, fine.' He let out a long breath. 'We need to secure the boat.'

'Batten down the hatches?'

'Exactly.'

'Um…what does that mean, exactly?'

Chase rolled his eyes. Millie smiled. Even though a storm was coming, even though they were at an emotional impasse, she still loved being with him. Loved how he could always make her smile.

'You can close all the portholes and stow any loose items in a safe place—there's a chest at the end of the bed. I'll pump the bilge dry.'

Millie had no idea what *that* meant, but she hurried to obey Chase's instructions. The first raindrops splattered against the porthole in the galley as she closed it. She threw a bunch of books and clothes in the fixed chest Chase had mentioned, and then went back on deck. The wind had picked up and Millie felt its bite. She thought vaguely of all the news reports of deadly tropical storms and hurricanes she'd read or listened to over the years and suppressed a shiver of apprehension. Judging by Chase's expression, they were in for a wild ride.

'What now?' Millie asked, raising her voice so Chase could hear her over the wind.

'You keep the bilge dry and I'll keep us steady so we take the waves on the bow. I've located our position and we're about twenty minutes off St Julian's. I don't want to get any closer until the winds die down. The last thing we want is to founder on the rocks.'

'Right.'

Chase showed her how to pump the bilge, and as the wind picked up and the waves began to crash over the bow they worked in silent and tandem focus. Millie was too intent on her job to feel the fear that lurked on the fringes of her mind. She was soaked and cold, the silk dress plastered to her body. Several times the boat rocked and she fell over, jarring hard. She looked back at Chase and saw him at the tiller, soaking wet and steady. Strong. Even in the midst of this fierce storm her heart swelled with love.

Millie didn't know how long they remained there, keeping the boat afloat and steady as the winds howled and the waves broke over the bow. At some point Millie realised she was needing to pump less and the boat wasn't rocking so much. The storm, she realised, had passed over them.

As the sea around them began to calm, Chase turned around to give Millie a tired smile. He looked haggard, the strong angles of his face and body almost gaunt with tension.

'We did it,' he said and Millie smiled.

'So we did.'

'Thank you.'

She nodded, her throat tightening. Now they were back to the argument that had seen them locked in battle, but at least she would fire the next shot. 'We seemed to weather that storm pretty well.'

Chase narrowed his eyes. 'I'd say so,' he agreed neutrally.

Millie took a breath. 'And if we can manage to do that, then—'

'We can weather the storms of life?' He rolled his eyes. 'Scary, are you really going to go there?'

She took a step towards him. 'I'll do whatever it takes, Chase.'

He gazed at her with a quiet kind of sorrow for a moment. 'I know you will. That's what worries me.' He sighed and stared out at the now-placid sea. 'Come below. We should change into dry clothes.'

Millie followed him below deck and changed into a spare tee-shirt and shorts of his while he did the same. Dry and tense with anticipation, she watched as he sat down on the edge of the bed and patted the empty space next to him. Not exactly the move of a seducer.

On jelly-like legs, Millie walked over and sat next to him.

Chase took her hand in his. Millie tried not to gulp. He was going to make her cry again, she thought numbly, and this time it wouldn't heal. It would hurt.

'Millie.'

'Don't give me the let-me-down-gently speech, Chase. We're both too tough for that.'

He gave her a small smile instead. 'You're right. You're strong, Millie, and incredibly stubborn.'

'Don't forget scary.'

'And severe. A lot of S-words there.' He sighed, sliding his fingers along hers, as if even now he just enjoyed the feel of her. 'You're tough enough to take the truth.'

She bristled, readied for battle. 'And which truth is that, Chase?'

'The truth that since my diagnosis my platelets have been falling. I'm still in the chronic phase of CML, but if you did your internet search then you know that once you hit the accelerated phase it's not good. In fact, it's really bad.'

'There are no guarantees in life, Chase.'

'No, but it's a guarantee that, once I hit that phase, there's no turning back. It's simply a matter of time until I have a blast crisis, and from then on my days are numbered. And those days are hard. We're talking chemo, radiation, hospice, a long, drawn-out sigh towards the end. It's not pretty.'

She swallowed, visions of Chase growing weak and frail filling her head. 'I know that.'

'Here's some more honesty,' he said quietly. 'We had a very intense time. You especially, in telling me about Charlotte and your husband. You hadn't talked like that or cried like that since the accident, and it's bound to make you feel differently about me.'

'You think my feelings aren't real?'

'I'm saying there's no time to test if they're real. We go back to New York and start dating and in a week, a month, who knows, I'm in the hospital and all bets are off. That's not fair, Millie.'

'I should be able to decide.'

'Are you telling me you actually want that?' Chase demanded. He almost sounded angry now. 'You're prepared to be my damn *care-giver* when you barely know me? Waste what could be the best years of your life on someone who's running out of time? Not to mention to go through the whole grief thing again?'

She swallowed. Said nothing. Because, when he put it as bleakly and baldly as that, it did sound absurd. And awful. And for a heart-wrenching moment she wasn't certain of anything; she knew Chase saw it in her face, heard it in her silence.

'See,' he said quietly, and he sounded pained, as if her silence had hurt him. 'It's not going to work, Millie.'

And Millie, her heart turning over and over inside her, was afraid he was right. 'I want it to work,' she whispered, and he squeezed her fingers.

'Let's just remember what we had.'

She swallowed, her throat too tight for her to speak. And then with a sad smile he let go of her hand and went back on deck.

Three days later Chase was travelling first-class back to New York. He gazed down at the blueprint he'd been working on, the blueprint that had completely, completely absorbed him a week ago, but all he could see was Millie. Millie's soft, dark eyes and sudden smile. Millie leaning over as she lay on top of him and kissed him, that severe hair he now loved—just like he loved all of her—brushing his bare chest.

Forget about it, he told himself, and resolutely banished the image—just as he'd done three minutes earlier. Sighing, he shoved the blueprint away and raked a hand through his hair. Those last hours with Millie had been horribly awkward and yet so precious. After they'd sailed back to St Julian's, he'd moored the boat and walked her through the resort. Neither of them had spoken. They'd both known it was over, and now there was just the mechanics of departure.

'I'll leave your clothes at the front desk,' Millie had said, for she'd still been wearing his tee-shirt and shorts.

'Forget about it.' His voice came out rough, rougher than he intended, because it hurt to speak. It hurt to think. It shouldn't have hurt so much, because it was what he wanted, yet it did. It hurt, absurdly, that she had so readily agreed.

She nodded slowly, then came to a stop in front of an outdoor roofed corridor. 'My room's down here.'

'OK.' He nodded, unable to manage anything more. She blinked at him.

'Chase…'

He knew he'd break if she said anything more. He'd break and then they'd start on a desolate path he had no intention of taking either of them down. 'Goodbye, Millie,' he said, and without thinking—because he needed to touch her, to taste her once more—he drew her in his arms and kissed her hard on the mouth, sealing the memory of her inside him. Then he turned and walked away quickly, without looking back.

Now Chase reached for the blueprint once more. It was of a university library in New Hampshire, and he didn't have the entrance right. He wanted soaring space without being grandiose, and of course the building—as with all his buildings—needed to be made of local and renewable materials. The colour of the oak he was using for the shelving reminded him of Millie's eyes.

Damn. He pushed the blueprint away once more. No point

in attempting to work. At least in sleep he wouldn't think of her.

He'd dream.

Several days later Chase sat in the office of his haematologist while she scanned the results of the battery of tests he'd undergone as soon as he'd returned to the city.

'The good news?' she said, looking up, and Chase nodded. 'Your levels are stable.'

'And the bad news?'

'They're a little lower than I would have liked, but there could be a lot of reasons for that.'

'Like the fact that the new medication isn't working?' Chase drawled, and his doctor, Rachel, gave him a wry smile.

'Chase, I know there is a tendency to expect the worst-case scenario in these situations, as a kind of self-protective measure.'

Spare him the psycho-babble. 'It's been my experience that the worst case is what often happens.' Like his mother getting breast cancer and dying within six weeks. Six *weeks*. Or his dad dying of a heart attack before they could reconcile, before Chase had even *considered* reconciling. He'd been so busy trying to show his dad how little he cared and he'd thought he had so much time. Time to prove himself. Time to say sorry for being such a screw-up.

And most of all like meeting Millie when it was too late, when his days were most likely numbered. Yeah, the worst case could happen. Most times it did.

'This is not the worst case,' Rachel said quietly. 'Trust me. This inhibitor isn't working as well as I'd like, it's true, but there's another one we can try. And, while your levels have dipped, they're not rocketing in the wrong direction.'

'But lowering levels is a sign of an accelerated phase,' Chase said, and it was not a question.

Rachel sighed. 'It can be, *if* you are exhibiting several other factors.'

'Such as?'

'There would be cytogenetic evolution with new abnormalities.'

'I don't even know what that means.'

'The point is, just because one medication isn't working doesn't mean you've become unresponsive to all therapies.'

'But it's not good.'

'I still maintain that we diagnosed CML at a very early stage, and the statistics are extremely positive for patients with your profile.'

'But, ultimately, I'm not a statistic.'

'No, you're not. But neither are you a worst-case scenario.'

Chase drummed his fingers on the arm rest of his chair. He hated not knowing. He hated feeling like a ticking time bomb about to explode.

'Live your life, Chase,' Rachel said quietly. 'Don't live it in fear of what might happen.'

'What will likely happen.'

'I'm not saying that.' She reached for her note pad. 'I'm writing you a prescription for a different inhibitor. We'll monitor your levels closely, once a week for the next month, and see how we go.'

'Great.' More doctor's appointments. More wondering. Rather belatedly Chase realised he was acting like a total ass. 'Sorry, Rachel. It hasn't been the greatest day.' Or week, since he'd walked off that plane and into his barren life.

Rachel smiled sympathetically. 'Work going OK?'

Chase fluttered his fingers in dismissal. 'Fine.'

'Personal relationships?'

He smiled thinly. 'What personal relationships?'

Rachel frowned. 'You need people to support you through this, Chase.'

That was exactly what he didn't need. He hadn't told anyone at work about his diagnosis. He hadn't even told his brothers, because he doubted they really wanted to know. The three of them hadn't exactly been there for each other since his parents had died.

No, he'd only told Millie.

'It's fine,' he assured his doctor, even though it felt like nothing in his life was fine. Everything, Chase thought moodily, sucked.

'I know a holiday can make you feel a little behind, Millie, but this is ridiculous.'

Millie glanced up from her computer monitor where she'd been scanning the closing prices of the Hong Kong Stock Exchange. She'd invested one of her client's assets in some new technology coming out of Asia, and it was looking good so far. Very good. So why wasn't she happier?

'You like me to work, Jack,' she said, glancing back at the screen.

Jack sighed. 'Not sixteen-hour days. I pride myself on a tough work ethic, but yours borders on obsessive. It's not good for you, Millie. You'll burn out. I've seen it happen. It's not pretty.'

'I'm fine, and I'm happiest working.' *Lies.*

'How was the holiday, anyway?'

It had been two weeks since she'd returned from St Julian's. Two long, lonely weeks where every moment when her brain wasn't fully occupied with work she'd caught herself thinking of Chase. Dreaming of him, his touch, his smile.

It wasn't real. It was just five incredible days, that's all.

She'd told herself that a hundred times already, and she still didn't believe it.

'Millie?'

Belatedly she realised she hadn't answered her boss. 'My holiday? Oh, you know…' She fluttered her fingers. *Amazing.* 'It was fine.'

'Everything's fine, huh?'

'Yep.'

'What did you do?'

'What do you ever do on a holiday?' *Dive for conch. Make love. Cry in someone's arms.* 'Sunbathe, swim…' She trailed off, her gaze determinedly still fixed on the screen.

'I always pegged you as more of an active holidayer. I figured you'd learn to scuba dive or parasail or something.'

'Nope.'

'Millie.' Jack put his hand on her desk, distracting her from her blind study of the screen. She glanced up and saw how paternally compassionate he looked. And Jack never looked paternal, or compassionate. He was too driven for that, just as she was.

Was trying to be.

'What is it, Jack?'

'You OK? I mean, really OK? I know with what happened… You know…the accident…' Besides a heartfelt 'I'm sorry' at Rob's and Charlotte's funerals, Jack hadn't talked about her bereavement. She'd been giving off clear don't-ask-me signals, and he'd obeyed them. Everyone had. Easier all round.

So why was he asking now?

She must really look like she was losing it.

'Thanks for asking, Jack,' Millie said quietly. 'But I'm… OK. I'll always carry that sadness with me, but it's not as bad as it once was. It gets better every day.' That much, at least, was true. Ever since she'd confessed and cried in Chase's

arms, she'd felt lighter. Better. Grief never went away completely, but it was no longer the suffocating blanket that had
smothered her for so long. She could breathe. She was free.

She didn't have Chase.

It wasn't real.

It *felt* real. Lying awake at night, remembering how he
he'd touched her and made her smile, it felt all too heartbreakingly real.

'Well.' Jack cleared his throat. 'I'm glad you're OK. So
stop the sixteen-hour days, OK?'

Millie just smiled and clicked her mouse to the next page
of the report. She had no intention of stopping.

Stopping meant thinking, and thinking meant thinking
of Chase. And there was no point in torturing herself any
more than she had to.

A week later her sister Zoe phoned her during her supposed lunch hour—spent at her desk—and informed her she
was coming by for dinner.

'I'm kind of busy, Zo.'

'Exactly. I thought you'd come back from this holiday a
little more relaxed, Millie, but you're worse than ever.'

'Gee, thanks.'

'I'm serious. I'll be by at seven.'

Since it was Zoe, Millie agreed. Zoe had been the one
person she'd felt she could be almost real with after the accident. Zoe knew there had been tension between her and
Rob, although she didn't know the source. She'd understood
Millie didn't want to talk about Charlotte, and she'd never
pressed. She just came over and brought corn chips and fake
cheese, made margaritas.

Zoe buzzed up promptly at seven; Millie had got in the
door three minutes earlier. She was still in her power suit and
spiked heels, and Zoe raised her eyebrows at the sight of her.

'Raar. I bet men find that get-up *so* sexy.'

'That is so not the point.'

Zoe dumped her bag of provisions on Millie's sleek and spotless granite worktop. 'I know, but men are such weaklings. I bet all your work colleagues have fantasies about you unbuttoning that silk blouse as you murmur stock prices.'

Millie let out an unwilling laugh. 'Zoe, you are outrageous.'

'I try. So.' Zoe took out a bag of tortilla chips and spread them on a pan. 'What happened in Hawaii?'

'I went to the Caribbean.'

'Right.' She reached in the bag for a tub of bright-orange cheese product. Yum. 'So what went down there, Mills? Because something did and I'll get it out of you eventually.'

'No, you won't.' Of that Millie was certain. She had far more self-control than her fun-loving sister did.

'Was it a man? Some hot island romance?'

Millie watched as Zoe squeezed the cheese all over the chips, and thought of Chase telling her how low-brow her snack of choice was. Even now the memory made her smile. 'Actually, it was.'

'What?' Zoe looked up, astonished, and squirted fake cheese across the kitchen right onto Millie's pristine white silk blouse.

'You are so paying for this dry-cleaning bill.'

'Done. And you are so telling me what happened.'

'There's not all that much to tell.' Millie dabbed ineffectually at the bright-orange stain. She was already regretting her impulse to confide in her sister. Talking about Chase hurt too much.

'Did you actually get it *on* with some *guy*?' Zoe asked, so incredulous that Millie had to smile.

'I did.'

'Was he hot?'

'Totally.'

'I am totally jealous.'

'You should be.'

'So it was a fling? A holiday romance?'

'Basically.' Millie tried for insouciant and failed miserably. She turned away under the pretext of running water onto a cloth to dab on her blouse, but really to hide the tears that had sprung unbidden in her eyes.

And of course she didn't fool Zoe.

'Oh, hon.' She put one hand on her shoulder. 'What happened?'

'It's complicated.'

'Knowing your history, I'd expect that.'

Millie sighed. 'Let me tell you, I am pretty tired of complicated. And I'm tired of sad.'

'I know you are,' Zoe murmured.

Millie swallowed, blinked and turned around. 'He had some issues.'

'Oh no, not a guy with issues. You're better off without him, trust me.'

Millie smiled wanly. Zoe was infamous for dating toe-rags who left her on some pathetic pretext of how being hurt by their ex-girlfriends, or their mothers, or their first-grade school teachers had made them commitment-phobic. 'Not like that.'

'Then how?'

'He…' She paused, not wanting to reveal Chase's condition. It wasn't her secret to share. 'It doesn't matter. The point is, he didn't want to continue it because he didn't want me to get hurt.'

'That is so lame.'

'He meant it, though,' Millie said quietly.

Zoe shoved the pan of cheese-covered tortilla chips in the oven. 'Oh, really? Because when a guy says something about how he doesn't want you to get hurt, what he really means is *he* doesn't want to get hurt.'

'No—' Millie stopped suddenly and Zoe planted her hands on her hips.

'Am I right, or am I right?'

Could it be possible? Chase had seemed so sincere, so sorrowfully heartfelt when he'd held her hand and told her the truth. Mentioned words like *care-giver* and *hospice* and *blast crisis.* And she'd believed him, because she wasn't stupid; a future with Chase was scary. And uncertain. And yet even now, weeks later, it still felt like her only hope.

What if he'd sent her away because *he* was afraid? Because he wanted to send her away before she walked away on her own? Because he thought she wouldn't handle it, wouldn't *want* to handle it?

'You might be right, Zo,' she said slowly. 'I just never thought of that.'

Zoe peered in the oven to check on their chips. 'For a financial genius,' she remarked, 'you can be kind of stupid about some things.'

Millie had to agree.

CHAPTER TWELVE

MILLIE straightened the tight-fitting black cocktail dress and threw her shoulders back. Show time.

It had taken nearly two months to track down Chase. She could have found him sooner; she'd found his office address on the internet and she could have shown up there any day of the week. But she wasn't about to blunder into battle; she needed to do this right. And it had taken her that long to figure out just how that could happen.

Now she stood on the threshold of the lobby of one of Manhattan's boutique museums, this one dedicated to Swedish modern art. The result was spare, clean lines, a soaring ceiling and a lot of funky sculpture. And Chase, who had designed the museum's new conservatory on the top floor, was in attendance at this opening night party.

Millie had been to plenty of parties in the city. Rob had liked to work the Manhattan social scene, often stating that he accomplished more in one evening at a party like this one than a week at the office. Millie had enjoyed the parties they'd attended for the most part, but she hadn't been to one in two years. And she'd never gone alone.

More importantly, she'd never gone to one with the sole intent of seducing the guest of honour.

She took a deep breath and scanned the crowd for Chase. Time to start putting her plan into action.

* * *

Chase gazed around at the milling guests in their tuxedos and cocktail dresses—all black, which was practically required at dos like these. Normally he liked working the charm, enjoying the hors d'oeuvres and the low-grade flirting, but he felt only weary of it tonight.

Hell, he'd been weary of it for the best part of three months since he'd left Millie—and his heart—on St Julian's.

That sounded like a song, he thought moodily. A bad one. He took a sip of champagne. By all accounts he should be happy. The new conservatory was a huge success in art and architectural circles and, even more importantly, the new inhibitor Rachel had prescribed him was actually working. For how long, of course, no one could say, but she was happy with his levels and he felt physically better than he had in months. He was even allowed to drink.

So why was he still so miserable?

'Hello, Chase.'

Chase turned slowly, disbelievingly, at the sound of that familiar voice. He blinked at the sight of Millie, *his* Millie, standing there so calm and cool, a flute of champagne held aloft.

'Aw, Scary, you changed your hair.'

Her lush mouth curved in the faintest of smiles. 'You didn't like it before.'

He took her in, *drank* her in, for despite her hair, which was now tousled and short, she looked so wonderfully the same. Same soft, dark eyes. Same lush mouth. Same straight, elegant figure clad in the kind of dress he'd expect her to wear—a black silk sheath with a straight neckline and cap sleeves, saved from severity by the way it highlighted every slender curve. His hands itched with the desire—the *need*—to touch her.

'How have you been, Chase?'

'Fine. Good. You?'

'The same, I'd say.' Her mouth quirked up at the corner, like she was teasing him. So he wasn't being the most sparkling conversationalist. All his energy was taken up with just looking at her. Memorising her. 'It's good to see you,' Millie said quietly and Chase nodded jerkily.

'You too.'

She raised one slender arm to gesture to the milling crowds, to the Manhattan skyline visible through the walls of glass. 'I like the space. Very open and modern.'

'Thanks.' He sounded like an idiot. A wooden idiot.

'I know you're the guest of honour here, but do you think you could be free for a drink at the end of the evening?' Vulnerability flashed in her eyes; he saw it, he felt it. 'For old times' sake.'

Chase knew it wasn't a good idea. What did he and Millie really have to say to each other? His new medication might be working, but he hadn't changed his mind about their future, or lack thereof. He was still a ticking time bomb.

And yet, one drink. Just to hear how she was. To be able to *look* at her. Nothing more. 'Sure.'

'Good.' Now he saw relief flash in her eyes, and he knew she still cared. Hell, so did he.

Maybe this was a bad idea.

'When will you be free?'

'I'm free now.' He'd already made his remarks, shaken the requisite number of hands. He was ready. *So* ready; maybe it would be better to just get this over with. Final closure.

Because that was what it really was, right?

'Well, let's go then.' And, turning around, Millie sashayed out of the conservatory. Chase followed.

They didn't speak in the lift on the way down, or out on the street when Millie raised one arm and had a cab coasting to the kerb within seconds. Chase didn't hear the address she gave as they climbed into the cab; he was too diverted by the sight of her long, stocking-clad legs. She was wearing *suspenders*, and he'd seen an inch of milky-white thigh as she slid across the seat.

His blood pressure was sky-rocketing. He could feel the hard thud of his heart, the adrenalin racing through his veins. He'd missed her. He'd missed her way too much. And he wanted her right now.

'Where are we going, out of interest?' His voice, thankfully, hit the wry note of amusement he was going for.

'My apartment.'

Brakes screeched in his mind. 'What?'

She gave him a far too innocent smile. 'Why waste twenty bucks on two glasses of wine in a noisy, crowded bar? This is much more civilised.'

And much more dangerous. Was Millie *playing* him? He'd always thought her too blunt to be sneaky, but maybe not. What did she want out of this evening?

What did he?

They didn't say anything more until the cab came to a stop outside a luxury high-rise near the UN complex. Chase reached for his wallet but Millie had already swiped her card.

'My treat,' she murmured and, swallowing hard, he followed her out of the taxi and into the lobby of her building, all black marble and tinted mirrors.

She fluttered her fingers at the doorman and then ushered him into the lift. Tension was coiling in Chase's body, seeking release. Something was going on here, some kind of plan of Millie's, and he didn't know what it was.

He had a feeling he was going to find out pretty soon.

She didn't speak until she'd reached her apartment, unlocked the door and led him into just the kind of place he'd expected her to have. Very tasteful. Very boring.

'Before you ask, an interior decorator did the whole thing. I didn't have time to go antiquing.'

'Still pulling sixteen-hour days, Scary?'

'More or less.' She took a very nice bottle of red out of a wine rack in the ode to granite and stainless steel that served as her kitchen. 'This OK?'

'Fine, but let me, or I'm going to start to feel surplus to requirements.'

She handed him the bottle and a corkscrew. 'Trust me, Chase, you are not surplus to requirements.'

'What's going on, Millie? Besides a friendly drink?'

'I have a deal to offer.'

A deal. Of course. He wasn't even surprised and yet his blood still sang. The cork came out with a satisfying pop and he poured them both glasses. 'What kind of deal?'

'One night.'

His hand involuntarily jerked, and a blood-red drop of wine splashed onto the counter. Millie swiped it and then licked the wine off her thumb. Chase went hard. 'What do you mean, one night?' he asked in as mild a voice as he could manage. Millie didn't answer, just accepted the glass he handed her and took a sip. 'Cheers,' he said and tried not to drain his glass.

Millie drank and then lowered her glass, gazing at him straight-on. 'One night—my terms.'

Hell. 'Which are?'

'Need-to-know basis only, of course.'

Of course. 'Why are you suggesting this, Millie?'

'Because I can't get you out of my head. It's affecting my work, my life—what little there is of it. And I'm gambling that it's been the same for you.' He didn't answer, which was obviously answer enough. 'One night, Chase, that's all. To help us get each other out of our systems and move on.'

He almost asked if that was what she wanted now, but stopped himself. What was the point? It was what he wanted. It had to be.

'And if I don't agree?'

'Stay and enjoy a nice glass of wine with an old friend.'

And *that* sounded so appealing. 'And if I do agree?'

Her mouth curved. 'Need-to-know basis, remember?'

'Is this some kind of revenge?'

'Revenge?' She let out a low, husky laugh. When had Millie become such an accomplished seductress? So unbearably sensual? 'Definitely not. Consider it…returning the favour.'

He swallowed. Stared into his wine glass. Wondered why the hell he wasn't busting out as fast as he could. This was dangerous. Stupid. Insane.

And he wanted it. So badly. Just one night. One more time with Millie.

'All right, Scary. I agree.'

'Even without knowing what you're getting into?'

'I think I can handle it.'

'Funny,' she murmured. 'That's what I thought when I first met you. Boy, was I wrong.'

She set her wine glass back down on the work top and walked past him towards the living room. 'Where you going, Scary?'

She glanced over her shoulder. 'To the bedroom, of course.'

Adrenalin pumped through him. 'That's kind of quick.'

'The only part of the evening that will be.'

Good Lord. Chase closed his eyes. This was the stuff of fantasies, of his dreams, for the last three months. He followed her into the bedroom.

The shades were drawn against the night, the king-sized bed covered with a pale-blue duvet that matched the curtains and carpet. The room was as tastefully boring as the rest of the apartment, but with Millie standing in the middle of it—her hands planted on her hips; one long, lovely leg thrust out as her gaze roved over him—it felt like the most erotic chamber he'd ever entered.

He shut the door behind him and leaned against it. 'Well?'

'Take off your clothes.'

He heard the slightest tremble in her voice and knew she wasn't quite the confident seductress she'd first seemed to be. Somehow that made him glad.

'Will do,' he drawled, and tugged off his tie. Millie watched him, her gaze dark and hot as he undid the studs of his shirt and cummerbund and tossed both on the floor. He raised his eyebrows. 'Well?'

'The trousers too, hotshot.'

He slid out of his trousers and kicked them off; his boxers and socks followed. He was naked and fully aroused while Millie was still in her clothes, even her high heels.

She looked him up and down and then lifted her honest, open gaze to his. 'I missed you, Chase.'

Chase didn't say anything. She was investing this night with emotion, emotion he felt. This was so dangerous. And exciting. He couldn't have walked away even if he'd wanted to. She nodded towards the bed. 'Get on there.'

Smiling a little, he stretched out on the bed just as she once had, hands behind his head, the image of someone totally at ease. Tension still raced through him. He didn't know what Millie planned, but he knew it was something. He could tell by the set of her shoulders, that glint in her eyes, the sense of expectation that pulsed in the room.

What was she going to do to him?

In one fluid movements Millie unzipped her dress and stepped out of it.

'I see you've bought some sexy lingerie since we last saw each other,' Chase said, and had to clear his throat.

Millie smiled. She was wearing a black satin bra and matching thong, and those suspenders. Sheer black stockings encased her lovely legs. She put one foot on the bed and slowly, languorously, rolled the stocking down her calf. Chase watched, mesmerised. Then she did the same with the other leg and stood up, the stockings held in her hand, the black lace suspenders discarded.

'Is this some kind of striptease thing? Because I like it.'

'I'm so glad,' she purred, and then leaned over him. Chase was so distracted by the close-up of her high, firm breasts encased in black satin that he didn't realise what she was doing with those sheer stockings. And when he did realise, it was too late.

'You tied me up.' One hand to each bed post.

'That's right.'

Chase pulled one hand, tested the weight of the bind. She'd tied a good knot, but he could still break out pretty easily. He wasn't going to, though. He was too intrigued by what Millie intended to do.

She ran one fingertip down the length of his chest, across his hip, and then down his inner thigh. His reaction to that little touch was, in his rather exposed and vulnerable state, completely obvious.

She stood up, hands on her hips, and Chase arched his eyebrows. 'What now, Scary?'

'You'll see.' She reached behind her for something long and silky. 'Or, actually, you won't.'

She was blindfolding him. Chase remained passive as she tied the scarf around his eyes, still too curious to stop this little game. 'You didn't ask if this was OK with me, you know. You're not being very PC about this.'

'I didn't want to ask,' Millie replied. 'There's no getting out of this, Chase.'

For the first time actual unease prickled between his shoulder blades. He kept his tone light. 'What are you going to do to me, Millie?'

'Make you tell the truth.'

Chase stiffened. 'The truth?' he repeated neutrally, because suddenly this didn't seem like such a sexy little game anymore.

'Yes, the truth.' He could tell by the sound of her voice that she was walking around the bed, and he felt more exposed than ever. 'Because it's taken me this long to realise you weren't telling me the truth when you said how you didn't want me to go through all the heartache of losing someone again, blah, blah, blah. Yawn, yawn, yawn.'

He managed a smile. 'You are reducing my heartfelt sensitivity to something rather trite.'

'It wasn't trite,' Millie said, and he knew she'd come closer. 'It was a lie.'

And Chase couldn't think to respond for a moment because she'd straddled his hips, lowered herself onto his thighs. He could feel the damp heat of her and she brushed against him so he actually moaned.

'You're torturing me here, Millie.'

'That's the idea.'

She moved again, so her body brushed against his in the most agonisingly exquisite and intimate of sensations. Chase scrambled to think of something coherent.

'Why do you think I was lying?'

'Maybe,' Millie said thoughtfully, 'you didn't realise you were lying. You'd convinced yourself you didn't want to hurt me.'

She leaned forward so her breasts brushed his chest, trailed a few lingering kisses along his shoulder. Thinking anything sensible was nearly impossible.

'I didn't want to hurt you,' he managed, his voice strangled. 'I still don't.'

'No, Chase,' she said softly, and her breath fanned against

his bare skin. 'You didn't want to hurt yourself. You still don't.'

For the first time Chase considered freeing himself, ending this farce. What the hell was she talking about? Then he heard the tear of foil and felt her slowly roll a condom onto him. His breath came out in a shudder as she lowered herself onto him.

'Millie—'

'I didn't see it at first,' she said, setting a slow pace that had him arching instinctively upwards. 'How you needed to lose control as much as I did.'

Somehow he found the strength to speak. 'I think I'm seconds from losing control right now.'

'Not that kind of control.' He heard amusement in her voice and she slowed the pace, rocking her hips just a little. 'But I want to spin this out a bit longer, so bear with me.'

Chase cursed. Millie laughed softly. 'Now, now, Chase.'

'Do you know what you're doing to me?'

She rocked her hips again. 'I sort of think I do.'

'What do you want, Millie?'

'I told you—the truth.'

'I gave you the truth.'

'No. The truth, Chase, is that you aren't afraid of leaving me alone. You're afraid of *being* alone. You're afraid I wouldn't be able to hack it and I'd walk away, leave you to suffer by yourself. Break your heart.' As she spoke she'd started moving again, setting a faster and faster rhythm so her voice was soft and breathless and Chase couldn't speak at all.

He could only listen, which he knew was exactly what she wanted.

'Hurting you just like your mother hurt you by dying when you were only a boy. Like your father, by never forgiving you and disinheriting you. Like your brothers, by not caring enough even to ask what's going on in your life. You gave me all the pieces of the puzzle, Chase, but I was so wrapped up in my own pain that it took me too long to fit it all together.'

Feeling blazed through him. Too much feeling. He was on the brink of the most intense orgasm he'd thought he'd ever had even as his heart started to splinter. *Shatter.*

Because she was right.

'Millie!' he gasped, her name torn from him.

She leaned over him, freed his hands and took off his blindfold. Chase blinked back sudden tears as she cradled her face in his hands, her expression so tender and fierce and loving. 'I'm sorry for not getting it sooner. I'm sorry I waited so long.' She kissed him long and deep. 'I'm not going to leave you, Chase. I'm not going to leave you even if you're sick and scared and dying. We have something special, something amazing, and I'll fight for it for the rest of my life.'

Then she kissed him again, still moving on top of him, and with a shudder of joy he came, his arms around her, drawing her even closer to him.

He was never going to let her go.

Some time later, after more love-making and honest words, Millie lay in his arms as Chase stared up at the ceiling. His mind and body still buzzed with everything that had happened. 'You know,' he said, running his hand up and down her arm, 'that was so not the deal we made.'

'It was better,' she murmured, and snuggled closer.

And Chase had to agree. This deal was much better. In fact, it was perfect.

EPILOGUE

Four years later.

MILLIE gazed out at the tranquil aquamarine sea and gave
a sigh of pure contentment. She could hear Chase in the
kitchen of the villa, humming as he made dinner for the
two of them.

They'd come to St Julian's to celebrate the fifth anniver-
sary of his diagnosis, a red-letter day, because his doctor had
declared him officially in remission. As of now, he had the
same life expectancy as a person without CML, which was to
say, who knew how long? Who knew how long anyone had?

There was just this moment. This happiness. And enjoying what they'd been given for as long as they'd been given it.

The last four years hadn't been without some fear and
heartache. Right after their wedding, his symptoms had
played up and his doctor had prescribed a drug that was
still in clinical trials. Thankfully, it had seemed to work.

Chase had told his brothers about his condition, and several years ago they'd had a reckoning, a reunion. Millie
would never forget the wonder and gratitude she'd seen in
Chase's eyes when he'd embraced the brothers who had
rallied around him even though he'd secretly feared they
wouldn't.

'It's almost ready,' Chase called, and Millie smiled, her hand resting against her still-flat tummy.

She had something else to be happy about, something secret and precious and scary too. Something she hadn't yet told Chase about, because she hadn't even been sure how she felt about it. It had taken four years to get to this moment, this willingness to risk so much again.

She felt ready now; being with Chase had given her the strength, the courage, to try, even while knowing that there were no guarantees. Life was scary, uncertain and full of pain. But it was also full of hope—glorious, prevailing, strong.

'Sweetheart?' Chase called and, smiling, ready to tell her secret, Millie rose from the sand and went to her husband.

* * * * *

Mills & Boon® Hardback

November 2012

ROMANCE

A Night of No Return	Sarah Morgan
A Tempestuous Temptation	Cathy Williams
Back in the Headlines	Sharon Kendrick
A Taste of the Untamed	Susan Stephens
Exquisite Revenge	Abby Green
Beneath the Veil of Paradise	Kate Hewitt
Surrendering All But Her Heart	Melanie Milburne
Innocent of His Claim	Janette Kenny
The Price of Fame	Anne Oliver
One Night, So Pregnant!	Heidi Rice
The Count's Christmas Baby	Rebecca Winters
His Larkville Cinderella	Melissa McClone
The Nanny Who Saved Christmas	Michelle Douglas
Snowed in at the Ranch	Cara Colter
Hitched!	Jessica Hart
Once A Rebel...	Nikki Logan
A Doctor, A Fling & A Wedding Ring	Fiona McArthur
Her Christmas Eve Diamond	Scarlet Wilson

MEDICAL

Maybe This Christmas...?	Alison Roberts
Dr Chandler's Sleeping Beauty	Melanie Milburne
Newborn Baby For Christmas	Fiona Lowe
The War Hero's Locked-Away Heart	Louisa George

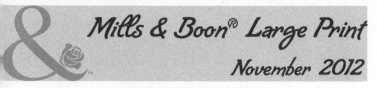

Mills & Boon® Large Print

November 2012

ROMANCE

HISTORICAL

MEDICAL

Mills & Boon® Hardback

December 2012

ROMANCE

A Ring to Secure His Heir	Lynne Graham
What His Money Can't Hide	Maggie Cox
Woman in a Sheikh's World	Sarah Morgan
At Dante's Service	Chantelle Shaw
At His Majesty's Request	Maisey Yates
Breaking the Greek's Rules	Anne McAllister
The Ruthless Caleb Wilde	Sandra Marton
The Price of Success	Maya Blake
The Man From her Wayward Past	Susan Stephens
Blame it on the Bikini	Natalie Anderson
The English Lord's Secret Son	Margaret Way
The Secret That Changed Everything	Lucy Gordon
Baby Under the Christmas Tree	Teresa Carpenter
The Cattleman's Special Delivery	Barbara Hannay
Secrets of the Rich & Famous	Charlotte Phillips
Her Man In Manhattan	Trish Wylie
His Bride in Paradise	Joanna Neil
Christmas Where She Belongs	Meredith Webber

MEDICAL

From Christmas to Eternity	Caroline Anderson
Her Little Spanish Secret	Laura Iding
Christmas with Dr Delicious	Sue MacKay
One Night That Changed Everything	Tina Beckett

Mills & Boon® Large Print
December 2012

ROMANCE

Contract with Consequences	Miranda Lee
The Sheikh's Last Gamble	Trish Morey
The Man She Shouldn't Crave	Lucy Ellis
The Girl He'd Overlooked	Cathy Williams
Mr Right, Next Door!	Barbara Wallace
The Cowboy Comes Home	Patricia Thayer
The Rancher's Housekeeper	Rebecca Winters
Her Outback Rescuer	Marion Lennox
A Tainted Beauty	Sharon Kendrick
One Night With The Enemy	Abby Green
The Dangerous Jacob Wilde	Sandra Marton

HISTORICAL

A Not So Respectable Gentleman?	Diane Gaston
Outrageous Confessions of Lady Deborah	Marguerite Kaye
His Unsuitable Viscountess	Michelle Styles
Lady with the Devil's Scar	Sophia James
Betrothed to the Barbarian	Carol Townend

MEDICAL

Sydney Harbour Hospital: Bella's Wishlist	Emily Forbes
Doctor's Mile-High Fling	Tina Beckett
Hers For One Night Only?	Carol Marinelli
Unlocking the Surgeon's Heart	Jessica Matthews
Marriage Miracle in Swallowbrook	Abigail Gordon
Celebrity in Braxton Falls	Judy Campbell